Love
&
SEX
ten stories of truth

Love

&

SEX

ten stories of truth

EDITED BY MICHAEL CART

SIMON PULSE
New York London Toronto Sydney Singapore

First Aladdin Paperbacks edition January 2003
Love and Sex: Ten Stories of Truth copyright © 2001 by Michael Cart
Foreword copyright © 2001 by Michael Cart
"Snake" copyright © 2001 by Laurie Halse Anderson
"Extra Virgin" copyright © 2001 by Joan Bauer
"The Welcome" copyright © 2001 by Emma Donoghue
"Fine and Dandy" copyright © 2001 by Louise Hawes
"Watcher" copyright © 2001 by Angela Johnson
"The Acuteness of Desire" copyright © 2001 by Michael Lowenthal
"The Cure for Curtis" copyright © 2001 by Chris Lynch
"Lightning Bringer" copyright © 2001 by Garth Nix
"Secret Shelf" copyright © 2001 by Sonya Sones
"Troll Bumps" copyright © 2001 by Shelley Stoehr

ALADDIN PAPERBACKS
An imprint of Simon & Schuster
Children's Publishing Division
1230 Avenue of the Americas
New York, NY 10020

Also available in a Simon & Schuster Books for Young Readers hardcover edition.
Book designed by Jennifer Reyes
The text of this book was set in Stone Informal.

Printed in the United States of America

2 4 6 8 10 9 7 5 3 1

The Library of Congress has cataloged the hardcover edition as follows:
Love and sex: ten stories of truth / edited by Michael Cart.
p. cm.
Contents: Extra virgin / Joan Bauer—Fine and dandy / Louise Hawes—
Lightning bringer / Garth Nix—Secret shelf / Sonya Sones—Snake / Lousie
Halse Anderson—The cure for Curtis / Chris Lynch—The acuteness of desire /
Michael Lowenthal—Troll bumps / Shelley Stoehr—Watcher / Angela Johnson—
The welcome / Emma Donoghue

ISBN 0-689-83202-6 (hc)

1. Short stories, American. [1.Sex—Fiction. 2. Short stories.] I. Cart, Michael.
PZ .L83 2001
[Fic]—dc21   00-052269

ISBN 0-689-85668-7 (pbk.)

*For my courageous editor, David Gale,
with gratitude and friendship.*

CONTENTS

Foreword by Michael Cart   ix

"Extra Virgin" by Joan Bauer   1

"Fine and Dandy" by Louise Hawes   21

"Lightning Bringer" by Garth Nix   45

"Secret Shelf" by Sonya Sones   63

"Snake" by Laurie Halse Anderson   89

"The Cure for Curtis" by Chris Lynch   109

"The Acuteness of Desire" by Michael Lowenthal   129

"Troll Bumps" by Shelley Stoehr   159

"Watcher" by Angela Johnson   183

"The Welcome" by Emma Donoghue   195

FOREWORD

by Michael Cart

More than thirty years ago a pioneering young adult librarian named Margaret A. Edwards protested that "many adults seem to think that if sex is not mentioned to adolescents, it will go away."

As succeeding decades have demonstrated, silence is no arbiter of behavior. Not only has sex not gone away, it has become a quintessential—perhaps even obligatory?—rite of passage for adolescents; 75 percent of young Americans now experience sex by the age of twenty. As for silence, it became a graver issue in the 1980s with the advent of AIDS and the realization that sometimes silence equals death. And yet it is still true, as Edwards further noted in 1969, that "too many adults wish to 'protect' teenagers when they should be stimulating them to read of life as it is lived."

Perhaps that is why there are still too few works of fiction for young adults that deal artfully yet honestly with the complexities of human sexuality and how they affect "life as it is lived."

I didn't discover Edwards's words until the mid-1990s, when I was doing research for a critical history of young adult literature. As I went on to do more research, I discovered that Edwards's words had stuck in my subconscious mind like a nagging grain of sand and were gradually turning into the pearl of an idea: Why not do a book about this?

The idea might never have become reality, however, had it not been for the fact that in 1995 I saw a movie titled *Kids*. It is photographer Larry Clark's lacerating directorial debut and features a screenplay by Harmony Korine, who was himself a kid, only nineteen years old at the time. The movie takes us inside the lives of a group of New York City teenagers who are sexually active—hyperactive, some might say. Clark's film has the cinema-verité look of in-your-face truth. But is it?

Frankly, I didn't want to think so. For these teens seemed to be trying to fill up the emptiness of their alienated lives with sex. Lots of sex. But in their version the mechanical act was everything; their sex was filled with impersonality, leaving no room for intimacy. It was not about sharing, it was about self-satisfaction, about conquest, about implied violence directed at the partner. There was absolutely no demonstration of caring, no evidence of engagement, no evidence of, well, love.

For an incurable romantic like myself, watching this film was a cold-shower experience. Did what I was seeing on the screen represent the real life of real teens, I wondered? Was this how their life was really lived today? Again, I didn't want to think so. And so I've done a lot of reading since then in search of answers and have discovered there is no shortage of empirical data about adolescent sexuality, but data, too, is soulless, heartless, and—here's that word again—loveless. The more I thought about the subject, the more I found myself wondering about the equation between sex and love in adolescent life and coming up with more questions than answers.

And so I turned to art, since I am a great believer in finding answers there—and not only answers but wisdom; wisdom to inform both the mind and the heart. My idea for a book finally turned into an invitation to ten wonderfully artful writers to create stories that address, in all their complexities, the interrelationships of love and sex.

In the collection that has resulted you will find stories about

Michael Cart

abstinence and obsession, about heterosexuality and homosexuality, about gender and transgender, about confusion and certainty, about fantasy and reality, about hurt and healing. And you will discover that the writers have approached their themes with gravity and grit, with humor and heart, with poetry, art, and—always—truth.

Joan Bauer, for example, wrote "Extra Virgin," a tender, funny story about an eighteen-year-old girl whose commitment to abstinence is tested when the man of her dreams walks into her life and whispers, "I want you so much." What choice will she make then?

In "Fine and Dandy" Louise Hawes also tells a story about choice and how one decision involving sex may lead to another, more difficult one, and how such domino-tumbling decisions change us—and others whose lives touch ours—in profound, sometimes heartbreaking ways.

Australian author Garth Nix recounts a story that at first seems quite different, a richly imagined fantasy about a strange man called the Lightning Bringer. And yet this story about sexual power also involves a choice that dramatically demonstrates how a boy's decision about his own surprising abilities will change his very real life.

Sonya Sones, whose first book, *Stop Pretending*, was a novel in verse, now gives us a short story in verse. Each poem in "Secret Shelf," her story-suite of verses, marks another step in Sophie's journey to emotional coming-of-age. Some of these verse-steps are sweet, some are passionate, and some are surprising, as Sophie discovers certain differences between lust and love.

Laurie Halse Anderson's "Snake" is a witty story about two teenagers who, on their first date, are surprised by temptation at California's Venice Beach and find themselves literally wading into an ocean of desire.

In "The Cure for Curtis" Chris Lynch writes an antic, amusing story about lust, love, and confusion as a teenage boy named Curtis desperately, turbulently tries to come to terms with his secret dreams—and his ideas about sexual identity.

"The Acuteness of Desire," by Michael Lowenthal, is also about sexual identity, a heart-touching story about a gay teen named Jesse who loves the precision, the absoluteness of geometry but who discovers, when he is assigned to tutor Matt, that love is messier and far less precise than mathematics.

Shelley Stoehr's "Troll Bumps" is not about mathematics but about music and a girl named Grace who is on the road, traveling across the country in pursuit of her musician boyfriend. How will her quest change her as she learns that love is sometimes like a song obsessively heard one too many times?

In "Watcher" novelist Angela Johnson also writes a haunting, dreamlike story about a search for love that takes two teenagers to the border of obsession.

And Irish writer Emma Donoghue writes in "The Welcome" a sometimes serious, sometimes satirical story that is also, in part, about obsession, as a young woman becomes fascinated with another young woman who has just moved into their cooperative house. But it is also a searching story about the walls of sexual identity that impose barriers between us.

So here, then, are ten very different stories. Indeed, their differences dramatize how varied and complex the intersections of love and sex are. But the stories also have something in common: a courageous, nonjudgmental commitment to telling the truth. Of course, sometimes the truth makes us uncomfortable, especially when it involves something as personal as sex—or love.

But, like Margaret A. Edwards, I think it is important to read of "life as it is lived." And so I urgently hope these stories will be read

Michael Cart

with open minds and hearts, and that they will then spark thoughtful and open discussion about "life as it is lived." Because that is how books—like this one—can change and even save lives. That is how wisdom begins.

In the meantime, as these stories clearly demonstrate, sex is not going away—but, then, neither is love.

A portion of the money generated from the sale of this book will be donated to the American Library Association's Young Adult Library Services Association (YALSA) for the promotion of books recommended by YALSA and of teen reading, including their national Teen Read Week.

So I'm working the late shift at *The Ice-Cream Man Cometh* on Twelfth and Luther. It's the first hot day of May, and we're busy. We've got big problems, too, because the freezer was on extra cold all day and all the gallons of ice cream have turned glacial. People are ordering double scoops tonight because everyone's in a festive mood due to the weather. My right arm feels like it's going to break off from digging into the Mocha Java. I need an ice pick to dent it. I've got a spasm in my neck from the stress, but the show must go on. I'm smiling for the customers. People don't want to think that their ice-cream server has any problems whatsoever.

I look up to see the growing line of ice-cream lovers.

And that's when *he* walked in.

Extra Virgin

by Joan Bauer

It had been a really long week, sexually speaking.

On Monday I had to walk past a construction site and hear four overweight construction workers whistle, belch, and make base comments about my anatomy.

On Tuesday Billy Grummond wore a "Coed Naked Ice Hockey" shirt to school and got sent home, but not before he asked me if I wanted to play on his team.

On Wednesday my cousin Biff came over and watched a TV show with my brother, Alex, about bikini-clad, big-busted blondes who hang-glide. There were lots of close-ups during takeoff and landing.

On Thursday, at our weekly extended-family dinner, over which I had toiled selflessly making lasagna, Biff held up the bottle of olive oil when my parents were out of the room and said, "Why do they call it extra virgin anyway?" He broke up laughing. So did my brother.

I decided to give him the technical answer. "Because it's made from the first pressing of the olives, you moron."

"That don't sound like no virgin anymore to me."

Snort, snort.

On Friday I had a blind date with Leonard Flicker. All that can be said of the experience is that if there was ever a reason to sign up for lifetime virginity, Leonard was it.

I confess that I come to the whole issue of sex as an irritated observer. On the one hand, my parents tell me it's the most wonderful thing that can happen between married people. And you know what? I believe them. On the other hand, I don't like the way society usually deals with it, don't like how certain people can make such idiots of themselves when the subject comes up, don't like advertising that's always shoving sex in my face to get me to buy something, like everyone in my generation can only and forever think about one thing.

If that is totally true, explain to me, *please,* how anyone ever gets into college.

Now, I admit that in the blooming department I am a late bud. I was still in a T-shirt when all my friends were in bras. I was just getting into flossing when everyone I knew got their first kiss. Regarding guys, I am fussy (there are *far* worse things). But you can't just decide one morning you're going to wake up and lower your standards.

Leonard Flicker springs immediately to mind.

In school we talked about abstinence and safe sex. I am definitely in the abstinence corner. All the facts on teenage pregnancy and sexually transmitted diseases scare me. But there's another thing too. I really want to wait until I'm married. That's the right decision for me. I've heard people say that abstinence will be hard to hold on to at times, but

I've shrugged that off. When you date guys like Leonard Flicker, abstinence is not a rough road to travel—it's a six-lane interstate highway.

So I'm working the late shift at The Ice-Cream Man Cometh on Twelfth and Luther. It's the first hot day of May, and we're busy. We've got big problems, too, because the freezer was on extra cold all day and all the gallons of ice cream have turned glacial. People are ordering double scoops tonight because everyone's in a festive mood due to the weather. My right arm feels like it's going to break off from digging into the Mocha Java. I need an ice pick to dent it. I've got a spasm in my neck from the stress, but the show must go on. I'm smiling for the customers. People don't want to think that their ice-cream server has any problems whatsoever.

I look up to see the growing line of ice-cream lovers.

And that's when *he* walked in.

Tall—about six two; dark hair; a day's beard—the planned kind. He was wearing jeans and a black T-shirt. His arms were muscled, but not like he spent all day lifting barbells. He was alone, mysterious, reading the flavor board.

I felt energy hit my face and flow through my hands into my powerful pink scooper. I was boring through the Double Fudge Delight, sprinkling miniature marshmallows on a little kid's sundae.

Barley Millforth, my co-worker, was doing his Darth Vader voice to amuse three girls, who were giggling. Everyone in line was laughing. Darth Vader hissing deep,

"One scoop or *two*," is pretty funny.

Mystery Male played it cool.

He turned to face the counter and looked directly at me. Our eyes locked. I swear.

Barley was moving down the line taking orders. I helped three more people, trying to time it just right so I could wait on this guy who kept watching me.

I could feel his eyes staring deep into the barrel of Blueberry Madness as I dug powerfully with my scooper, plopped one scoop into a cup, handed it to a large woman.

He was in front of me now.

Barley as Darth asked him, "What can I get you?"

A total invasion of my space.

He said, "I'd like *her* to help me," in this low, craggy voice.

And I nearly keeled right there because low and craggy has always hit a major chord with me.

I raised my scooper. "You can't win, Darth. If you strike me down, I shall become more powerful than you could possibly imagine."

Mystery Male laughed and ordered Coconut—two scoops in a cup—which was wonderfully distinctive.

He ate it at a table, watching me. He was there until closing. He asked if he could buy me coffee, which I never drink, and I wasn't sure if I should go, because I didn't know him.

"Just across the street," he said, and I went. I knew the owner. It was safe.

We talked until 2 A.M. about absolutely everything. His

name was Cal. He was a freshman at Penn State (one town over), staying for the summer semester. He hadn't chosen a major yet but was leaning toward computer science. I hated telling him I was still in high school—but I was a senior, an eighteen-year-old senior (i.e., functioning adult), and I emphasized that twice. I told him about how I was going to Rutgers for the fall term and I was interested in sociology, which didn't seem to turn him off, unlike most guys, who at the mere mention of sociology look at me as though I've just passed gas.

"So what group in society do you find the most interesting?" Cal asked. A finely etched question. I told him about my term paper on immigrants and the struggles they faced in a new land.

"And what does this tell me about you?" he asked, smiling.

A male who had in-depth thoughts.

"I think it says I'm not afraid of challenges, and when I make a decision, I stay committed to it. That's what immigrants had to do."

"That's a good way to be," he said.

We talked about music and art and traveling. We closed down the coffee bar.

I called my mom three times so she wouldn't worry.

"Can I see you tomorrow?" Cal asked.

Absolutely.

Then he kissed my hand. I swear. And it wasn't in a lame way; it was natural, like you'd expect a steamy actor to do it and leave some poor girl in a blob on the street.

"I'll see you tomorrow." My voice was an octave lower.

That's how it began with Cal and me.

And it went on like that for a while. We'd meet and have coffee. He'd ask great questions. I'd forget to order decaf and would be awake for hours into the night.

"If you could have dinner with anyone living or dead, who would it be?" he asked me one night.

I ran through my list. "William Shakespeare . . . no . . . Winston Churchill . . . no . . . Margaret Mead . . . no Eleanor Roosevelt . . . no . . . Nancy Drew . . ."

He laughed. "A great American."

"Who would you choose, Cal?"

He took my hand. "I'd choose you."

We grew closer and closer. We saw each other every day. Our kissing got deeper—there was a fire to it.

I was feeling things I'd never felt before, feeling terribly mature, and pretty young at the same time. Once when we were kissing deep, he called me "my Beth." No one in my life had ever called me that. Hon, yes. Sweetie. Miss. Mrs. Ice-Cream Lady—a little girl shouted that once. *"Elizabeth!"* the parental voice thundered when I was bad.

But never my common old name with a personal pronoun in front of it.

Now, *my mother.* She's a very sensitive person. She can tell when a storm is coming. The National Weather Bureau has yet to discover her powers. And she was getting more and more sensitive every time Cal came to the door. She'd look at me with X-ray vision when I came in from a date, her maternal eyes boring a hole into my heart, which was probably open and throbbing on my sleeve.

A knock one night on my bedroom door.

Mom's there looking nervous. She comes in, sits on the bed.

"I want to talk to you about Cal."

Groan.

"I sense you're on complicated ground with him, Beth, maybe for the first time in your life."

I looked down. "I'm handling it."

"I know what it's like to be there. It's hard to pull away when you want something so much."

It seemed strange she was saying this.

"I want you to be honest with me, honey, about what's happening." She searched my face. "We haven't had a talk about sex for a while."

"Mother, the last time was when we watched that video with the dancing sperm."

She laughed. "They weren't dancing."

"There was disco music, Mom. Remember, the egg was kind of gyrating."

Mom covered her face. "This is what you remember."

"You don't have another bad video you want us to watch, do you?"

"No. I just want to remind you of how these things—"

"—can backfire. I'm in control, Mother."

"Honey, it's best not to let yourself get into situations where one thing might lead to another."

"Don't you trust me?"

"Yes. I do. But it's good to talk about these things, Beth. It's good to remember what to do, what you believe, and how to not let things get out of hand."

"I know all this, Mother."

But now a week later . . .

"Beth." He breathed it heavily in my ear. "I want you so much."

Those words.

We were in his dorm room—a bad move, I know. I hadn't really wanted to come here, but somehow here I was. His roommate was gone for the weekend. At first we sat on his bed eating chips and salsa. Then Cal pushed the chips out of the way, put the bowl of salsa on the shelf above his bed. We lay down, which took a real commitment because his college dorm bed was short and narrow. It had probably been picked out by mothers who were trying to make these situations as difficult as possible. Cal started kissing me, and it didn't take long before I felt my resolve slipping. He rubbed his body into mine. I felt heat in places that had heretofore remained at room temperature. My skin was just tingling and my brain was somewhere else. And when Cal took my face in his hands and kissed me deeper than I thought possible, when he told me that he loved me in that low, craggy voice, when his hand stroked the back of my leg, something about that just made me wild with wanting him.

"Let me show you how much I care, baby."

I was finished.

Electric shocks were hitting everywhere in my body.

He threw the pillow on the floor, rolled me on my back and directly onto the bag of salted tortilla chips, which had scattered during our tumble. I felt the whole Muchas Grande sixty-four-ounce bag and its strewn contents go *crunch* underneath me.

Few people think about this in the heat of passion, but tortilla chips have very pointy edges.

For me, this lightened the mood, but Cal was dead serious about moving forward.

"I have chips digging into my back." I said this tenderly.

He reached for the bag and hurled it across the room. "I've got a condom."

"There's a tortilla particle lodged between my shoulder blades."

He flailed for it. "Okay, okay, I'll get it."

And I guess between the crunch of Mexican food and my Catholic-school upbringing, which basically taught you that at any moment, day or night, no matter where you are or what you are doing, three nuns could jump on the scene and start screaming at you, I embraced this visual and found the resolve to say, "Cal, we need to stop."

I pushed him gently away.

He wasn't getting the idea.

"We're just getting started." He went back to kissing my neck, brushing crushed tortilla pieces from the bed.

"No, Cal, this is too much."

"Beth, you feel so good."

"Cal, no. We've never talked about this."

"Don't talk." A huge deep kiss.

God.

I was sinking, feeling a hundred things at once. But I knew someplace distant that I wasn't ready for this.

"Cal, I can't go to bed with you."

I managed to sit up, which was when I found the salsa, or rather it found me. Toppled from the shelf above the bed, just missing my head, landed in a plop of red, chunky muck right there on the striped sheets.

Not exactly three screaming nuns, but it worked.

I reached to turn on the light—knocked it over, actually—at which point Cal uttered an extended series of four letter words, but that was good because it broke the hold of the moment.

I sat there shaking.

He sat there with his shirt opened, breathing hard, looking absolutely gorgeous despite the mess around him.

"I'm a virgin." I said it louder than I meant to. Like I was trying to convince myself.

Cal was trying to catch his breath. "Okay . . ."

"And I'm not ready to go to bed with anyone. I mean, I've made a decision sort of . . . not sort of . . . I've made a decision to wait . . . you know . . ."

"Till when?"

"Well . . . till I'm sort of . . . married."

He lay back on the bed, put his arms under his head. "Sort of married?"

Joan Bauer

"I mean definitely . . . married . . . in years to come."

If I didn't die first from sounding stupid.

He opened a Coke, propped himself up, took a swig, said nothing.

I picked up the lamp that had fallen. It was casting a weird glow over the Muchas Grande salted tortilla chip bag. That bag had probably saved me. I'd never thought of Mexican food as having that kind of power.

I shook the crushed chips from my back, my hair. It was so clear to me that I'd almost gone to bed with him. It would have been so easy to do it.

"I . . . I shouldn't have come here, Cal."

Still silence.

I touched his hand. "I care for you very much."

He nodded. Got up, buttoned his shirt. "I'll take you home."

A long walk to the Volvo.

Car doors shutting, safety belts locked.

No great questions. Nothing to tell me he cared.

Silence in the car.

My house loomed. The front-porch light beamed. Mom had gotten a brighter bulb when I started going out with Cal. My brother, Alex, joked about how it attracted low-flying aircraft.

"I'll call you, Beth." Flat voice.

No you won't.

I slumped up the walk feeling totally alone.

"You're not alone," Sister Angelina would have told me. "You have your principles."

I always hated it when she said that.

He drove away.

Bye, Cal.

I walked in the house.

My mother, of course, imagined the worst. "Oh, God, what happened?"

"Nothing."

"Look at you!"

I looked at myself in the mirror. Face splotched. Mouth kind of swollen. Hair disheveled.

"Beth, you can tell me anything, you know that."

"Buy tortilla chip stock, Mom. It's going to go through the roof."

"What are you talking about?"

"I didn't go to bed with him, *okay*? I wanted to, but I *didn't*!"

I ran up the stairs as my great-aunt Minerva walked out from the kitchen, drop jawed.

I ran down the hall, into my room.

Flopped on my bed.

Looked at the phone. I wanted it to ring. I wanted Cal to call so I could tell him everything I was feeling—how much I probably loved him, how turned on he made me feel. I wanted to tell him that I wasn't a prude or some frozen female. I wanted to go to bed with him as much, maybe, as he wanted to go to bed with me.

I wanted to find the right words, like they had in the brochures that I'd read at school, where couples had great conversations about this and no one ever got hurt. I knew that waiting was the right decision. Cal was close to becoming my best friend, and now I had two losses to deal with.

Tears ran down my face.

I'm sorry that you couldn't let me be myself, Cal.

I'm sorrier about that than you'll ever know.

A postcard from my cousin Dana was on my pillow. My mother had put it there probably. Dana had gotten married last month and moved to Seattle. The postcard said simply, HOW GOES THE BATTLE?

Dana was my example in life and abstinence. Whenever anyone gave me a hard time about my stand, I'd point to Dana—a twenty-eight-year-old, attractive, popular, successful person who had just gotten married as an official virgin.

"We don't know that for sure," said my cousin Margaret at the wedding. "I mean, we can't drop her in the lake and see if she floats."

"Virgins float?"

"You know what I mean. Like Ivory soap."

Dana's wedding was wonderful. I thought of her in her long dress; the surety on her face. What I loved about Dana was that she was never self-righteous about her decision. She knew lots of people didn't agree with her. She just quietly lived her life, making the choices that were right for her beliefs.

A knock on the door.

Extra Virgin

The lady or the aunt?

I threw my pillow on the carpet. It couldn't get worse.

"Come in."

It was my mom, taking in the scene. I looked really pitiful.

"Are you okay?"

"No."

"I think it's brave what you did, Beth."

"I don't feel very brave."

"I know." She sat on the bed.

"Did . . . Aunt Minerva hear . . . what I said?"

"Every word."

"I thought she was hard of hearing."

"So did I."

We laughed.

I picked up Dana's postcard. It was like a lifeline to what I hoped to be.

Mom looked like she did whenever she was going to say something really major—i.e., give a speech. She was rustling around in her pocket, looking for something. All month long she'd been bringing out my baby pictures; she'd even kept all of my baby teeth, for crying out loud. Laid them out in little plastic bags for me to look at. This happens when you're about to graduate.

But she just sat with me, not saying anything.

Which was exactly what I needed.

June 14. Two days after my high school graduation. I'm

at The Ice-Cream Man Cometh, waging war against a fierce tub of Banana Butter Brickle. So far today work has been a yawnfest because it's raining like a monster outside and people don't think of treating themselves with little cold goodies in the middle of a monsoon. One customer in the place—a middle-aged woman. Barley's going strong with Darth Vader: "Would you like whipped cream *and* nuts on that sundae?"

"Why not?" said the woman nervously. Not a *Star Wars* fan.

"As you wish, my master." Deep, galactic breathing.

I was in the back lugging jars of butterscotch out from the stockroom.

"Beth . . ." It was Barley. "We got busy all of a sudden."

"Coming." I spilled the butterscotch on my apron, my hands.

Rushed back out.

Barley pointed at Cal, who was standing there smiling.

"Double Coconut," he said. "I missed you."

I felt two things simultaneously.

Caring and caution.

He held out his hand. I didn't take it right away. I did finally. Got him real sticky with butterscotch. This is how it goes in the ice-cream world.

"I want to talk about things, Beth."

I swallowed. "Okay."

Darth: "Something tells me there will be a sequel."

"We could go for coffee when you get off," Cal offered.

Barley said I could take a half hour now if I wanted—no one would be coming in that he and the Dark Side couldn't handle.

Cal opened the front door for me. We walked to the coffee bar across the street. Past the magazine stand displaying X-rated covers. Past a poster of a model in underwear flagging down a taxi. Past a big sign that read JUST DO IT. Past a movie theater placard with a man and woman kissing passionately underneath the grabber headline THEY COULDN'T SAY NO TO THE FIRE THAT RAGED WITHIN THEM.

It's lonely in this old world sometimes.

We sat at the table where we first sat six weeks ago.

"Okay." Cal leaned forward. "What was the worst part for you this last month?"

That was easy. "Feeling like you were only going out with me for one thing. What was it for you?"

He looked at me sadly. "Knowing I'd been a jerk when I took you home after . . ."

"The dorm incident."

"The dorm incident." He put his hand out. "Can we try again, Beth?"

"I'm not going to change, Cal."

"I figured. That immigrant strength of yours. I meant can we try again with your rules? I'll respect where you're at. I promise."

This was sounding a lot like the brochure they'd passed out in school.

I searched his face like my mother searched mine.

He laughed. "Do you want me to sign something?"

I grinned. "Maybe."

He picked up a napkin, took a pen, wrote, "Abstinently yours, Cal Fedders."

"Date it," I said, grinning.

He wrote "June 14th," gave it to me.

I folded it and put it in my pocket. I'd have it plasticized later for my mother.

"Are you hungry?" he asked.

"Starved."

"Mexican food?"

We looked at each other, shook our heads.

"A cuisine that doesn't crunch," I suggested.

We had a really nice Italian dinner at Pellicci's down the street, and when the waitress put the bottle of extra-virgin olive oil on the table, we both started laughing.

"You want butter instead?" she asked.

"No," Cal assured her and me. "This is right."

about "Extra Virgin"

This is a story that took me, the writer, on a journey. I'm always slightly irritated when I hear people talk about how easy certain choices in this world can be. On losing weight: "Just stop eating." On being less stressed: "Simply learn to relax." I've always found in my own life that when I try to set boundaries, I usually have to think them through again and again, and sometimes I must put them to a test to really make them stick.

Now, in the big sexual arena in which we live, abstinence isn't always the most popular choice and can be considered prudish and boring. We live in a sex-driven culture, where sex is used to sell everything from motor oil to makeup. But I know many young people (and older ones too) who are choosing to wait. I wanted to write a story about a girl who had chosen abstinence for a number of reasons and then had to put it to the test when she met a guy she went crazy over.

"Extra Virgin" is a story about choices. But it's also a story about the pervasive sexiness of our culture and how that affects the way we see ourselves as human beings. I greatly admire my eighteen-year-old character, Beth, because she sets boundaries, learns from her mistakes, and grapples with the issues even when it hurts to do so. When I wrote the scenes with her mother, I felt like her mother. It's not always easy to talk about sex with a teenager, and adults feel the struggle too. We feel inept sometimes, downright dumb. But you know how it is with fiction writers—we put so much of our personal self into a story. Maybe I *am* Beth's mom. I like to think so.

Joan Bauer

about Joan Bauer

Joan Bauer's first published piece of writing was a poem, "Lima Bean Blues," which won second prize in the *Chicago Tribune Magazine*'s Fruit and Vegetable Poetry Contest. Following careers in sales and advertising, journalism and screenwriting, she wrote her first young adult novel, *Squashed,* while recovering from a serious automobile accident. It won the Delacorte Prize for a First Young Adult Novel and has been followed by five additional novels: *Thwonk, Sticks, Rules of the Road* (which won the *Los Angeles Times* Book Award and the Golden Kite Award), *Backwater,* and *Hope Was Here,* a Newbery honor book.

Joan Bauer lives in Connecticut with her husband and daughter.

It was the day of rose number four that I knew for sure. I'd never missed a period before, but I didn't let myself worry for three weeks. Then I bought a test kit at a Rite Aid two towns over and sneaked it home. It was the kind with a plus for pregnant, a minus for not, the kind you see advertised on late-night TV. I got a plus. I figured I'd done it wrong, so I did it again. I didn't cry when I found that last rose, and I didn't cry when I got the second plus.

Fine and Dandy

by Louise Hawes

I'm too heavy for my height. I have a temper that can strip paint and a hammertoe like my father's. So when Pratt Nolan called me perfect, I wasn't even tempted to believe him. But that was Pratt's style, always trying to please, always making the best of things. And yes, always pretty boring.

So why did I go out with him for nearly a whole year? Because no one else asked me and because, quite honestly, it takes a while to get tired of being perfect. Especially when your mother and your stepfather are so wrapped up in their autumn romance they hardly notice anyone else. When they make it obvious they'd much rather spend evenings out with each other than baby-sit you.

Which is why my mother's voice turned to syrup and went up a whole octave every time Pratt came to the house. She even started buying snack food, something she'd never done before, something she'd maintained for seventeen years would "ruin" my dinner. "I've put the dip and chips on the coffee table," she'd tell us, practically singing, grinning as if she expected a medal, as if she'd cooked us a five-course dinner. She'd slip her arm through Pratt's, then link up with me, too, posing for a picture that never got taken. "Now, you two have fun."

When my stepfather brought the car around and was sitting on the horn, she'd act as though she hated to tear herself away. She'd push money for pizza into Pratt's hand, then remind me about feeding the cat and getting to bed early. And of course she made sure we knew she wasn't going to have a good time. "I don't know why Earl insists on this party," she'd tell us, frowning, shrugging her sequined shoulders. "I told him it's just another B-and-B fest, booze and bores." But you should have seen her run once she was out the door, all clattering heels and whiffs of Shalimar trailing behind her.

So there we were, alone, perfect me and the first guy who'd ever looked at me. We'd start by renting a video or doing homework, but sooner or later every night ended up the same way: horizontal. "You're so beautiful," Pratt would say, jamming his hand down my V-neck and tugging at my bra strap. "Honest, Casey, you are so sweet."

Then he'd be all over me, and I'd be breathing hard, trying to slow things down so I'd remember what it felt like afterward. Pratt and I were both virgins, so I didn't worry about AIDS or anything. I guess that's part of the reason we finally had sex. It was safe, as safe as it was going to get. College would be different, I knew. What were the odds of finding a college guy who'd never done it?

Besides, it was good to have someone to go places with. Parties, movies, hanging out at Suds 'n' Pins—I didn't have to think about it anymore. I'd be there with Pratt. Casey and Pratt, Pratt and Casey, like bread and butter, yang and yin. Well, maybe more like puzzle pieces that were too weird to fit anywhere else. But trust me, it was a big relief. No more wondering if anyone would ask me to a dance, no more mooning around the house on weekends. No more whining about my nonexistent sex life to Alyssa.

Alyssa Hazlitt is my best friend and, unless you count my aunt Feather, the only one I tell stuff to. The trouble with talking about Pratt to Alyssa was that she's not at all like Feather, whose cheekbones are so hollow they'd catch rainwater and who has had a full, if tragic, love life. Alyssa's weight problem is worse than mine, and she's never been on a date in her life. She figured I was living a dream and had no right to complain. Much less break up with Pratt.

"Are you demented?" When Alyssa is outraged, she flushes and you can see little red blood vessels under her skin. When she's disappointed, she has this habit of biting her top lip and shaking her head. After I broke up with Pratt, I guess she was outraged and disappointed at once, because her face lit up like a viable alternative energy source and she shook her head back and forth, back and forth, like one of those dogs you see on dashboards. "Casey, have you totally lost your grip?" Shake. Shake. "He gave you a one-week anniversary present. Hello? One week!"

"I know," I told her, trying not to look at the teeth marks on her lip. Pratt liked to make celebrations of everything, and he'd left a rose in my locker after we'd been going out for a week. And a month. And six months. In fact, he was always giving me presents—silly things like a musical pen or a paisley teddy bear with K. C. on its stomach. "It's just that Pratt can be, you know, too much of a good thing."

"Too much of a good thing?" Shake. Shake. "What on earth is that supposed to mean?"

I thought for a minute. "Picture yourself all wrapped up in cotton candy."

Alyssa stopped shaking her head and started smiling. "So?"

"So you're inside all this sugar." She wasn't getting it, but I needed to tell her anyway. "You're looking out at the world through this pink goop, and you're dreaming every night about mustard, soy sauce, and salsa so hot it makes you cry."

"You're kidding, right?"

"He says I smell *yummy*, Liss. When I ask him how he is, he says *dandy!*"

It was true. The rest of us were closing in on the future: Our computers talked out loud and performed surgery; we owned TV screens as big as football fields and cell phones the size of postage stamps. But Pratt sounded like none of it had happened. Like he was still on a wagon train bound for the promise of the West. He had his girl beside him, he was spitting into the wind, and everything was *dandy*.

Until we rented *Madame Bovary*. We'd signed up to do a joint book report for English. It was due the next day, and Pratt hadn't even started reading. I'd almost finished, so I knew Emma Bovary was going to get bored with her husband and have affairs. What I hadn't realized, though, until I saw him fleshed out on my TV screen, was how much Dr. Bovary reminded me of Pratt.

"What'd I do to get so lucky?" Pratt asked it right after the credits, his voice soft as purring. I had helped him get my jeans down to my knees, and now his hands were between my legs. I liked the way the dim light from the TV made my thighs look thinner, and I liked what Pratt's hands were doing, but I wondered why he always decided to tell me how special I was just when I wanted to close my eyes and not think about anything at all. Then, right in the middle of trying to concentrate on the good feeling and block out Pratt's purr, I heard Emma Bovary's husband. "I am the most fortunate of men," he said. "What did I do to deserve you, my dear?"

That's when I remembered the part of the book where Emma wishes her husband would beat her, because at least that way she wouldn't feel guilty about hating him. And I remembered how she waited every day for happiness, like a white sail in the distance, to come closer.

So I broke up with Pratt. I put the VCR on pause, turned to him, and said, "I'm not as nice as you think I am." I pulled my jeans back up and turned on the light.

Pratt's eyes are green, but so dark they sometimes look black—like the skin of an avocado when it's too ripe to cut into pieces but perfect for guacamole. I'd spent the last eight months with those lightless veggie eyes fastened on me. Now they blinked, then fastened even harder. "Don't you dare say that, Casey Windsor. You are the smartest, sweetest person I know." His voice dropped from a purr to a whisper. "And that includes my mom."

I wondered if it was because I was his first girlfriend, because he wanted to make sure I wouldn't disappear, that he was always watching, whispering. "Pratt," I said, "we're both going away to college next year, right?"

"You are, for sure." He grinned at me proudly. "The way my GPA looks, I'll have to stay right here and go to State." He squeezed my hands, then rubbed them between his like they needed warming. "But we'll write every day, and you'll come home weekends."

Maybe, I decided, it wasn't just because I was the first person he'd ever had sex with. Pratt would probably stare at his next girlfriend too, probably follow every bite she took while they ate fries, study every move while she zipped her jacket or opened the mail. That's just the way he was. "Look. I think we should see other people."

Anybody else but Pratt would have wondered *what* other people. I wasn't exactly Homecoming Queen; I knew, if Pratt didn't, that I'd go right back to spending Saturday nights with Alyssa. To making my mother feel guilty when she and the life of the party left us behind.

"Gee." I swear it, Pratt actually said "gee." Only it was longer and sadder, more like, "Geeeeee."

"I don't want to see anybody but you," he told me. I'd managed to get one hand free, but he was still rubbing the other harder than ever, his avocado eyes filling up. "And you know what, Case? I don't think I ever will."

He phoned every day for a week, then every week for a month. And he left four more roses in my locker. But even though it would have been easy to fall back into seeing him, I decided it wouldn't be fair. I mean, Emma Bovary talked herself into marrying her country doctor, but she didn't have my advantage—she didn't know how much she was going to regret it.

"You did the right thing." My aunt Feather was a lot more help than Alyssa or my mom when I started staying home weekends again. "It's a very short trip from boredom to irritation." She finished the last of the white-chocolate brownies we'd made one Saturday night, then licked the crumbs from her fingers. "And an even shorter one from irritation to hatred. Why should somebody who adores you have to put up with that?"

I'd finished my brownie some time ago and was considering going back for the mixing bowl. "Mom is really disappointed." I studied my aunt's slender wrists, decided against the bowl. "She says I shouldn't set standards no one can reach."

"There's nothing wrong with high standards," Feather said. "*Somebody* in this family has to have them." I knew she didn't think much of my stepfather. I'd heard her try to talk my mother out of marrying him. It hadn't worked, of course, and now my mother was out dancing and my aunt was here with me. "Come on," she said, changing the subject too quickly. "Let's go put your hair up."

I loved the way I looked when she'd finished, my lank brown hair piled into a comb, long wisps trailing in front of my ears. I turned my head stiffly, afraid to topple the comb, watching myself in the mirror. The girl I saw was prettier, thinner, older. She looked a lot like Feather. From now on, I decided, narrowing my eyes and pursing my lips like someone in a perfume ad, I was going to grow up, not out.

"All you need is accessorizing." My aunt was looking at me too, her generous lips tucked into a pout. "Here." She took the silver chain from her own neck, hung it around mine. It was shorter on me than on her, so the charm nested in the space where my collarbones meet. "That's from New Mexico. Nice piece." Her pout turned into an approving smile. "It's right on you. Keep it."

I peered into the glass to get a closer look at the charm. It was a little silver woman with tiny children all over her. They were sitting on her stomach, perched on her shoulders, hanging from her hands, like burrs that had stuck to her and wouldn't come off.

"She's an Indian storyteller," Feather said. "I got it at the pueblo in Albuquerque." Cocking her stunning head, "Like?"

I nodded, fingering the little woman with her round, open mouth and her burr babies. My aunt had spent five years in the Southwest; she was always decked out in Indian silver—bracelets, rings, belt buckles, pins. They all looked dramatic and sexy against her olive skin, set off her blue eyes. "Thanks, Feather. Thanks a lot."

Louise Hawes

She leaned behind me, put her head beside mine as we peered into the mirror together. "Don't forget how pretty you look now, Cassandra. There's going to be a whole parade of male types, and they'll all be telling you what Pratt did. You don't need to take the first one that comes along."

It was the day of rose number four that I knew for sure. I'd never missed a period before, but I didn't let myself worry for three weeks. Then I bought a test kit at a Rite Aid two towns over and sneaked it home. It was the kind with a plus for pregnant, a minus for not, the kind you see advertised on late-night TV. I got a plus. I figured I'd done it wrong, so I did it again. I didn't cry when I found that last rose, and I didn't cry when I got the second plus.

I locked my door and lay on my bed, my hands over my belly, which didn't feel any bigger than it ever had. Or any smaller. Still, I wrapped my arms around it, like I was carrying myself, and stared up at the ceiling. I couldn't cry, because I couldn't believe it. I couldn't imagine there was someone else inside me, or the beginning of someone else. It didn't feel like there was room in there for another body, for a whole new set of arms and legs, another heart pumping along with mine.

Okay. Maybe you figure I got just what I deserved. Not only did I have sex with someone I didn't love, I had dumb sex. (That's the opposite of safe sex, according to Ms. Ciaccone, who is our Group Living and homeroom teacher, and who never really impressed me except by the size of the mole under her right eye, and maybe that's why I didn't really think it was dumb until it was too late.)

I'd always figured the mess we cleaned up afterward was all there was to it. That every one of the babies Pratt and I moaned and panted into possibility was trapped in the handful of sticky tissues I buried under orange peels and coffee grounds in the kitchen trash. It was a small price to pay for having someone to go to parties with, someone who actually liked the body I'd spent years hiding under baggy pants and extra-long flannel shirts.

I stared at the ceiling until dinner. Dry-eyed, I thought about college and about how much I wanted to get away from my family, my small school, my smaller life. I fingered the tiny baby bumps on the storyteller charm, and I thought about how I wasn't the only one who wanted me out of town. My mother was already counting the days until she and Mr. Bojangles could get back to their honeymoon. "Just think," she'd say, one braceleted arm against the door, her suede jacket draped over the other, "only one more month until you hear about colleges. Just half a year till I have to say good-bye to my brilliant, brilliant girl."

I tried to break the news to her while we ate leftovers she'd brought home from an Indian restaurant. My stepfather was working late, and it was just me, my mother, and a very small plate of kofta curry with brown rice congealed into microwaved gobs. "How old are you?" I asked.

"Not fifty, thank God," my mother said, separating her

rice with a plastic fork. "Why?"

"How old were you when I was born?"

"Let's see." My mother leaned back in her chair, grinning, challenged. She loves to talk about herself. "It was right after I'd lost that hideous job at Winchell's. Can you imagine? Pruning poodles like topiary! One little nick and they fired me. As though that beast even noticed. In fact, it adored me, slobbered all over my face, practically had to be dragged out."

I stared at her.

"I must have been thirty-two then," she decided. "Yes, thirty-two. Why?"

"Was I planned?" I pictured Pratt and me on the couch, our jeans around our ankles, the TV talking to no one.

"Planned?"

"You know. Did you want me?" Pratt would be a good father, I knew that. It wasn't Pratt I was worried about.

My mother's intrigued, interested look faded. "What a question, Cassandra Ann," she said. "I can't believe you could even ask me that."

And then I was picturing something else. It wasn't Pratt and me at all. It was me and Mom, before Prince Charming. I must have been twelve or thirteen, and I'd gotten this late case of chicken pox. I itched all over and my stomach ached and I was burning with fever. My mother sat next to me on the bed and brushed my hair while I was lying there. Gently, so it streamed out over the pillow. Gently, as if I were still a little girl, over and over. "Mom, what if I didn't go to college right away? What if I took a year off and then went?"

My mother laughed, shook her head. "Oh, no you don't, missy," she said. "You're not going to hang around this dumpy town a minute longer than you have to." She was sitting up straight now, paying attention. "You're not going to make the same mistake I did."

"But, I—"

"But, but, but. Forget *but,* Cassandra. I will not even hear of your putting off college. What do you think your father started that trust fund for? What do you think I've been dreaming of all these years?" She put down her fork, took my hand like she was campaigning for office. "I promise you one thing right now. You're going to college next year, and I'm going to Spain."

"Where?"

A flash of confusion, a nanosecond of apology. "Sure. Didn't I tell you?" Her eyes dropped away from me, lowered to her lap. "Earl knows how miserable I'll be without my baby girl, so he's taking me on a cruise. Barcelona." When she looked up, the guilt was gone. Her eyes were glowing, greedy. "Málaga, Valencia—that's where the oranges come from. Seville, Gibraltar. I'll shop myself stupid, I know I will." She paused, found inspiration. "And I'll bring my girl back something special too. Something useless and romantic and just for you."

If my pregnancy would throw a crimp in Mom's plans, it would have blown Alyssa's world apart. Only I never told her. Alyssa is a Catholic, a really good Catholic, and she didn't even know how far things had gone between Pratt and me. My descriptions of making out, how Pratt put his hands all over me, how I rubbed him until he was hard, always drove her crazy. "Stop," she'd say. "I can't hear another word. I can't." Then she'd giggle. "I am so jealous, Casey. I swear I am. But I'm glad I don't have to confess your sins. It's bad enough just telling Father Blainy I wish I was you."

"Alyssa!" The day she told me that, I grabbed her chunky wrists, squeezed them too tight. "You promised you'd never breathe a word to anyone." I squeezed harder. "You promised."

She pulled her hands away. "I didn't," she insisted. "I just told Father I have this friend, and that I've sinned by wanting to do the same lustful things she's done."

"Lustful things?"

Alyssa smiled, flushed. "That's church talk for the good parts," she admitted. Then she was giggling again, expectant. "So, what else? What happened next?"

I couldn't believe it was in the phone book. But it's right there in the Yellow Pages under *A:* ABORTION SERVICES. Anybody can look it up, can shop for it like a hair salon or an Italian restaurant. I wondered if SMUGGLING was listed under *S,* MARIJUANA FARMS under *M.* (They aren't. I checked.) I stared at the boxed ads that ran across three pages. "SAFE, AFFORDABLE, COMPLETELY CONFIDENTIAL." "REASONABLE RATES, COMPASSIONATE PHYSICIANS." "FRIENDLY OFFICE, CHOICE OF LOCAL

OR GENERAL ANESTHETIC." It sounded like they were selling shoes.

As usual, Aunt Feather ended up being the only one I could talk to. When I told her about the test and the phone book and how miserable I was, she hugged me. Then she asked me what Pratt thought about it. "I haven't told him," I said. "And I don't want to.

"He's not the one who'd have to give up college if I have a baby. He wouldn't have to go away somewhere so we don't embarrass Mom."

"Maybe your mother would surprise you," Feather said, though she didn't sound much like she believed it. "Or maybe Pratt would."

"Pratt wouldn't surprise me at all," I told her. I remembered how he used to talk about a family, how he always said he wanted two girls and two boys, just like his mom had. I told him I didn't think I'd ever want to have children, that I didn't even like my little cousins. "That's just because you're not ready yet," he'd said, like he was my father or something, like he'd been alive years longer than me. "When we're married you'll feel different."

So I knew I could have it. A church wedding with flowers, bridesmaids, the works. I knew Pratt would do the "right thing." In fact, I figured he'd be almost as happy as my mother, to have me settled, out of harm's way. He'd take me back and he'd be glad not to do more reports on books he hadn't read, to start right in working for his dad instead of going to State. Singing over the heads of those wagon

Louise Hawes

mules, hauling his wife and four kids along with him. Dandy. Just fine and dandy.

"The thing is," I told Feather, "I wish Pratt *would* surprise me." I told her how I couldn't bear the thought of marrying him, of having affairs, of waiting forever for that white sail. She didn't get it at first, but when I explained about *Madame Bovary,* she nodded. Then she hugged me harder.

"So you want to end this baby before it gets started?"

"That's just it," I told her. "I don't *know* when a baby starts." I remembered the ads, the shock of their cheerful borders decorated with curlicues and roses. "I wish I didn't have to think about it."

"But you do."

"It's only . . . I can't help wondering, what if Mom had decided not to have *me*?"

Feather nodded, smiled. "I don't think you'd have cared very much at the time."

I focused on my belly, tried to picture the tangle of neurons and blood vessels inside, imagined them clotting into a vague ball like the one we'd seen at school in *The Miracle of Birth.* It was Ms. Ciaccone's favorite film, so I'd seen it about forty thousand times.

"Want my slant on things?" Feather sucked in her pretty, hollow cheeks. "I know for sure you're alive, but I'm not positive about an embryo. You've got the equipment to suffer, but I don't know if that germ inside you does." She brushed my hair back from my forehead. "Any more than those little brown dots you find on egg yolks."

Fine and Dandy

I felt dizzy, sick. And suddenly worried about the brown dots. "But people who've been hypnotized," I told Feather. "Sometimes they, you know, go back to the womb. They remember the music their mother listened to, stuff like that."

"Casey Lamb, I don't know what to tell you." She was shaking her head. "What I hope is, souls keep trying until they find the right womb." She sighed. "They come back until somebody wants them."

"You mean, this baby"—a quick, instinctive hand on my stomach—"will get another chance to be born?" I imagined a nest of babies, one inside the other, like the wooden toys that split in half over and over, getting smaller and smaller, so you can fit them back together any time you want.

"That's what I mean," Feather said. "I guess you could say that's what I'm banking on." She sat down heavily beside me. "I had an abortion a long time ago, Case." She looked at me, or through me, to some place I couldn't see. "It seems like centuries."

"You?" I stared at my beautiful aunt. My bejeweled, sophisticated, forever cool aunt. "You?"

She nodded again. "I wasn't married, but I was in love, very much in love." She grinned. "And pregnant. Very pregnant."

I searched the past, trying to find the man Feather had loved. I remembered an officer, a banker, a whole parade of dark suits stooping down to me over the years. But none of them seemed special enough, worthy of my shining aunt.

"He died before you were born. And I guess I just didn't

care about having a baby without him. All the love got sucked out of me, you know?"

I didn't know. But I wanted to. Not the losing part, but the loving. I wanted to feel that someday. And I guess that's when I figured it out. When I realized that I didn't want a family until it happened. Until that white sail, billowed with yearning, got so close it blocked out everything else.

I couldn't sleep the night before Feather drove me to the clinic. I lay facing my digital alarm, watching the numbers change, the minutes blinking into hours, and I talked to the dot that wasn't going to grow into a baby. "Little germ," I told it, "I hope you understand about college and my mom and Pratt. I hope you'll come back when I'm ready. I'll take good care of you then, I promise. I'll watch my diet. I'll stop sneaking smokes. After you're born, I'll never leave you alone. We'll only eat leftovers once a week, and I'll brush your hair even when you're not sick."

If my life were a movie, there'd be a fade-out here; the screen would go dark and you'd never know for sure what I decided. You'd never see me and Feather in her battered Pontiac, nosing down the highway under a swollen sky. You wouldn't sit through our long gray drive across the state line to a place where you didn't have to be eighteen or have parental consent. You wouldn't see us pull into the parking lot just as the rain hit, or watch us scurrying toward the low-slung brick building, racing up the steps, and walking into a sudden, ridiculous riot of birthday party colors.

Fine and Dandy

Plastic chairs in red and green, orange and yellow, lined the waiting room. Two of the walls were painted light blue, the other two violet. On the receptionist's glass window was a smiley-face sticker with a note that said, DON'T WAKE ME, I'M SLEEPING ON THE JOB.

My life is not a movie; it's just a life. So I went through the whole thing, from start to finish. There was no dramatic scene where I thought things over, jumped up, and ran out of that room, determined to raise my baby against all odds. I didn't think or run, and I wasn't determined at all. I was numb. It was as if I'd brought the day inside with me, as if everything were happening behind a cloudy film.

I saw them and I didn't see them: the crinkly receptionist, who handed me a clipboard with a form to fill out; half a dozen girls my age, bent over movie and hairdressing magazines; a dark-haired woman who called everyone honey. "Honey, let's get you up on this scale." "That's fine, honey. You're not nervous, are you?"

Even if I'd wanted to change my mind, there wasn't much time. The Honey Woman talked to all of us together. "Now, girls," she said, "we need to make sure you understand what's happening." She read the form we'd all signed, but she read it so fast none of us could hear a word. One girl, with grape-colored lip gloss, looked up at me and smiled while the words sloshed over us like spray from traffic zooming by.

Then Feather kissed me and I was lying down and the Honey Woman was bending over me. "If you have any questions, anything on your mind, honey, just speak right up," and before I could answer, "Count backward from ten, honey. Everything's going to be fine."

And dandy, I thought, floating away, my arms and legs getting lighter and lighter, the anesthetic making me forget how to count. *Nine.* Maybe I said it, or maybe I only thought it. *Eight.* Then before I could figure out what came after eight, it was over. I woke up with a dream still in my head.

I was aware of the dream before I noticed the cramps. So first I was sitting on the ground, and I was wearing a long skirt that fell in layers like drooping petals. There was laughter and noise everywhere, and I was surrounded by little children. Some were sitting beside me, others were standing on my knees, their tiny arms wrapped around my neck, their grimy fingers twisted in my hair. Still others were trying to haul themselves up into my lap, grabbing fistfuls of my flower skirt, whining for attention. "Get away," I told them, angry at the dark spot of drool or tears that was spreading across my blouse. "Shoo! Scram!" I yelled, pushing them off. But they held on tighter, chattering, crying, choking me.

Then the dream was gone, and all I felt was the pain. It was like I was losing pieces of myself, like I was a continent and parts of me, whole panhandles and peninsulas, were being ripped off and washed away. Even groggy, I knew it wasn't true. I knew the dot had already been vacuumed out, just the way the dark-haired woman promised. But something was still under way, something that rushed and tore and hurt. Hurt like hell.

I took the pills they gave me, and my aunt drove me home. Mom and Attila the Hun were off learning to speak Spanish or line dance or something, so I crawled into bed without anyone asking me why I wasn't out having fun. Feather kept trying to mother me, piling books by my bed, making soup, fussing. She might as well have mothered a zombie. The pills brought the cramping under control, but they also made me groggy again. All I wanted to do was sleep.

I tried to lie on my stomach but felt puffed and achy. When I rolled over to one side, something pointed and small dug into my ear. It was the charm from my new necklace. I lifted my head, unfastened the catch, and poured the necklace into my palm, studying the coiled links, the tiny silver storyteller. She was a heavy woman, with thick, sturdy arms and a tulip-shaped skirt exactly like the one in my dream.

I lay back, fingering the charm, smoothing the plump baby knobs with my fingers. And that's when I started feeling sorry for somebody besides myself. That's when I remembered Pratt.

Feather had made me promise to tell him about the clinic. But when she asked me on the drive over if I'd talked to him, I just nodded. It wasn't exactly a lie, not a spoken one, anyway. Still, I never did say anything to him. I couldn't bear to start things up again, to have him thinking I wanted us to raise a child together. Somehow I'd never considered, not for a minute, that he might want to raise it all by himself.

Louise Hawes

And suddenly that's what I felt worst about. Because *I* would be all right. Sure, I'd have to endure the rest of the year, have to sit with Alyssa at school mixers, watching the guys who never ask anyone to dance, the soles of. their Timberlands propped up against the gym wall, crushed paper cups in their hands. But when the summer was over, I'd leave for college, too sad, too old for those boys anyway.

But what about Pratt? College didn't mean the same thing to him it did to me. And my nightmares were probably his dreams. Why shouldn't he have the chance to hover, to watch over someone who'd really appreciate it? Why wouldn't his nonstop love, his Velcro eyes, be just right for a baby? I thought about that, and the tears finally came. I don't know why, but once I started, I couldn't stop. It made me cry and cry to think how Pratt would have loved the drool and the noise and the tiny pincer hands; how he would have sat, rigid with pride, smiling like crazy, and just let those babies crawl all over him.

about "Fine and Dandy"

Not long ago, while a group of friends and I were white-water rafting, one of us fell overboard and was swept under the boat. A few seconds of clawing for daylight, of staring up at the black bottom of the raft, changed Karen—dramatically. Since she was hauled on board, waterlogged but safe, she's packed a lifetime's worth of growth into a few short years. She's stopped dreaming and started doing: She has moved from New York City to the West Coast, has given up a drone-type publishing job to work with troubled kids, and is making plans for her barefoot summer wedding to a man who may not live to see their children grown.

My point? Profound physical and emotional shock often changes us. Not gradually or even gracefully, but through sudden, unalterable kinetic and spiritual transformation. Such transformations are the stuff of stories, and if "Fine and Dandy" were about Karen's experience on the raft, or about someone contracting cancer, getting hit by a bus, or being tossed around by an earthquake, I would likely be safe from hate mail.

But I am not. My story describes an abortion, and abortion is different from other traumas: It is experienced only by women, and it is usually experienced under wraps. In a society casually familiar with violence, sex, and death, abortion may be our last taboo.

Some feminists have suggested that if men had to endure abortions, they would have been made safe long ago, and the instance of illegitimate births would have dropped precipitously. But we are *all* compliant in the conspiracy of silence that surrounds abortion. I know many families who have kept the secret of abortion over generations, families in which grandmothers, mothers, and daughters have each ended one or more pregnancies without telling a single male relative or anyone outside the family circle.

Aborting fetal life, like giving birth, involves emotional and

Louise Hawes

physical shock. It leaves most women who undergo "the procedure" deeply changed. They are unlikely ever to look at sex or their body or love or children in the same way they did before. They have had an epiphany, that moment of insight writing teachers and literary critics are so fond of pointing out in stories. These women have felt so much, come so far so fast, that they can never go back. Unfortunately, they are often too angry, too wounded, or too frightened to share what they have learned.

Yes, I will undoubtedly get hate mail about "Fine and Dandy." Abortion is still a place most people don't want stories to go. But I hope I will also hear from girls and women glad of a chance to break their silence, to talk about their own choices. And finally, I hope that some of the letters will come from male readers, who may not have heard about abortion from the women in their lives. If the voice of this story speaks to them, if it tells them the truth, that's a start.

about Louise Hawes

Louise Hawes teaches at the nation's first M.F.A. program in writing for children at Vermont College. She is the author of the middle-grade Nelson Malone books and of young adult novels, including *Rosey in the Present Tense.* She has earned two New Jersey State Writing Fellowships and the New Jersey Author's Award, and her work is represented in Prentice Hall's young adult fiction text *The Reader Writes the Story.*

Louise lives in North Carolina.

The guy looked like trouble. Then he smiled, and if you couldn't see the aura, that smile would somehow make you think that he was all right, the biker with the heart of gold, the drifter who went around helping out old folk or whatever.

But I saw part of the energy go out of his aura and into the smile, flickering out like a hundred snakes' tongues to touch and spark against the dull colors of the people around him.

He charmed them, that's what. I saw it happening, saw the tongues coming out and lighting up the older kids' gray days. And then I saw all the electric currents come together to caress one student in particular: Carol, the best-looking girl in the whole school.

Lightning Bringer

by Garth Nix

It was six years ago when I first met the Lightning Bringer, on a cloudy day just a few weeks past my tenth birthday.

That's when I invented the name, though I never spoke it, and no one else ever used it. Most of the townsfolk called him "Mister" Jackson. They didn't know why, but they called him mister, even though he looked pretty much like any other hard-faced drifter. Not normally the sort they'd talk to at all, except maybe to order off their property—once they were sure the police had arrived.

I knew he was different from the first second I saw him. It's like a photograph stuck in my personal album, that memory. I walked out the school gate, and there he was, leaning against his motorcycle. His jet-black motorcycle that looked like a Harley-Davidson but wasn't. It didn't have any brand name or anything on it. He was leaning against it, twice my height back then, because he was tall, easily six foot three or four. Muscles tight under the black T-shirt, the twin blue lightning tattoos down his forearms. Long hair somewhere between blond and red, tied back with a red-and-white-spotted bandanna.

But what I really noticed was his aura. Most people have dim, fuzzy sorts of colors that flicker around them in a pathetic kind of way. His aura was all blue sparks, jumping around like they were just waiting to electrocute anyone who went near.

The guy looked like trouble. Then he smiled, and if you couldn't see the aura, that smile would somehow make you think that he was all right, the biker with the heart of gold, the drifter who went around helping out old folk or whatever.

But I saw part of the energy go out of his aura and into the smile, flickering out like a hundred snakes' tongues to touch and spark against the dull colors of the people around him.

He charmed them, that's what. I saw it happening, saw the tongues coming out and lighting up the older kids' gray days. And then I saw all the electric currents come together to caress one student in particular: Carol, the best-looking girl in the whole school.

Of course, I was only ten back then, so I didn't really appreciate everything Carol had going for her. I mean, I knew that she had movie-star looks, with the jet-black hair and the big brown eyes, and breasts that went out exactly the right amount and a waist that went in exactly as it should and legs that could have been borrowed from a Barbie doll. But it was sort of secondhand appreciation at that stage. I knew everyone thought she looked good, but I didn't really know why myself. Now I can get really excited thinking about the way she looked when she was playing basketball, with that tight top and the pleated skirt . . . at least till I remember what happened to her. . . .

She was looking especially good that day. With hindsight, I reckon she'd found out that she was really attractive to men, picking up a certain confidence. That air of the cat that's worked out it's the kind of cat that's always going to get the cream.

When the Lightning Bringer's smile reached out for her, her eyes went all cloudy and she kind of sleepwalked over to him, as if nothing else even existed. They talked for a while, then she walked on. But she looked back—twice—and that electricity kept flowing out of the drifter, crackling around her like fingers just aching to undo the big white buttons on the front of her school dress.

Then she was around the corner, and I realized everyone else had gone. There was just me and the man, leaning against his bike. Watching me, not smiling, the blue white tendrils pulling back into the glowing shell around him. Then he laughed, his head pulled back, the laughter sending a stream of blue white energy up into the sky.

That laugh scared the hell out of me, and I suddenly felt just like a rabbit that realizes it's been staring into the headlights of an oncoming truck.

Like a lot of rabbits, I realized this too late. I'd hardly got one foot up, ready to run, when he was suddenly looming over me, fingers digging into my shoulders like old tree roots boring into the ground. Like maybe he'd never let go, till his fingers plunged through the flesh, squishing me like a rotten apple.

I started to scream, but he shook me so hard I just stopped.

"Listen, kid," he said, and his voice was scraped and raw, like maybe he'd drunk a bottle of whisky the night before, on top of a cold. "I'm not going to hurt you. You can *see*, can't you?"

I knew he wasn't talking about normal eyesight. I nodded, and he eased off his grip.

"I'll tell you something for free," he said, real serious. He bent down on one knee and looked me right in the eye, except I ducked my head, so I had only about a second of that fierce, yellow-eyed gaze burning into my brain.

"One day, you can be like me," he whispered, voice crawling with little lightnings, power licking away at my head. "You saw how that girl looked at me? I'm going to have her tonight. I can get any woman I like—or any man, if I was that way inclined. No one can touch me either. I do what I want. You know why? Because I was born with the Power. Power over things seen and unseen, power over folk and field, power over wind and water. You've got it too, boy, but you don't know what it can do yet. It can go away again if you don't look after it right. You've got to keep it charged up. You've got to use it, boy. That's the truth. You have to feed the Power!"

Then he kissed me right on the forehead, fire flaming through my skull, and I could smell my hair burning like a hot iron, and I was screaming and screaming and then the world spun around and around and I wanted to throw up

Garth Nix

but instead I lay down and everything went black.

When I came to, the Darly twins were turning my pockets inside out, looking for money. I was still pretty dizzy, but I punched one while I was still on the ground, and he fell back into the other one, so I got up and kicked them both down the street.

That made me feel better, and I thought maybe the worst of the day had happened and it could only get better from there.

But I was wrong.

I was real restless that night. Everybody was. The air was hot and sticky, with thunderheads hanging off on the horizon, black and grumbling but not doing anything about moving in to break the heat. There was nothing on television either, and we all sat there flicking between channels and complaining, till Mom lost her temper and sent everyone to bed. Including Dad, but he lost his temper too and they had a shouting fight, which was rare enough to send us shocked to bed.

I remember thinking that I wouldn't be able to get to sleep, but I did. For a while, anyway. I had this awful dream about the Lightning Bringer, how he was creeping through the house and up the stairs, blue sparks jumping around the bent-back toes of his boots. Then just as those lightning-tattooed arms were reaching down, fingers spreading around my neck, there was this incredibly loud burst of thunder, and I woke up screaming.

The thunder was real, drowning my scream and bringing a cold wind that rattled the shutters in counterpoint to the bright flashes of lightning behind them. But the rest was just a dream. There was no one there except my brother, Thomas, and he was asleep.

Still, it shook me up pretty bad. I can't think why else I would've gone to the window and looked outside. I mean, if you have a nightmare, normally that's the last thing you do, just in case you see something.

Well, I saw something. I saw the Lightning Bringer on his motorcycle, parked out in our street, looking right up at the window. He had Carol with him; her arms tightly wrapped his well-built, leather-clad chest. She had a bright red jacket on and jeans, and a red woolen hat instead of a helmet. She looked like the sort of helper Santa Claus might choose if Santa read *Penthouse* a lot.

The Lightning Bringer smiled at me and waved. Then he mouthed some words, words I understood without hearing, words that seemed to enter my brain directly, punctuated by the distant lightning.

"I can have anything I want, boy. And you can be just like me."

Then he revved up the bike and they were gone, heading up the road to the mountain, the lightning following on behind.

I never saw Carol again, and neither did anyone else. They found her a few days later, burned and blackened, her fabled beauty gone, life snuffed out.

"Struck by lightning," said the coroner. "Accidental death."

No one except me had seen her with the Lightning Bringer. No one except me thought it was anything but a tragic accident. She'd been foolish to go out walking in the thunderstorm, stupid to be out that late at night anyway. Some people even said she was lucky it was the lightning that got her.

I was the only one who knew she didn't have a choice, and it wasn't any ordinary lightning that killed her. But I didn't tell anyone. Who could I tell?

I'd like to say that I never thought of the Lightning Bringer after that day—and what he'd said—but I'd be lying. I thought about him every day for the next six years. After I got interested in girls, I think I thought about him every five minutes. I tried not to, but I just couldn't shake the memory of how Carol had looked at him. I wanted a girl like Carol to look at me like that, and do a whole lot more besides.

I used to think about the Lightning Bringer before school dances when I just couldn't get a date. Which, to be honest, was all the school dances up until about two months ago. Then I met Anya. Okay, she didn't look at me like Carol had looked at the Lightning Bringer, and she didn't look like Carol. But she was pretty, with sort of an interesting face and clever eyes, and she used to know what I was thinking without me saying anything. Like when I'd want to undo the back of her bra strap and just slide my hand around, and she'd shift just enough so I couldn't reach—before I even started to do anything.

Lightning Bringer

Which was frustrating, but I still really liked her. She had an interesting aura, too, a bit like apricot jam. I mean apricot jam colored, and quite thick, not like most of the fuzzy, thin auras I saw. I often wondered if she could see auras too and what mine looked like, but I was too embarrassed to ask her. Which was a bit of a problem, because I was too embarrassed to talk about sex with her either, and I knew that this was probably half the reason why she kept shifting around when I tried to put my hands places that seemed quite normal to go. And why she never let me kiss her for more than a minute at a time.

I mean, I think she would have if I'd talked to her about it. Maybe. Once I ignored her trying to pull away and I just keep kissing, sticking my tongue in even harder and putting my hands down the back of her jeans. Then she started jiggling about, and I thought it meant she was getting excited, till I realized it was sort of panic and she was just trying to get loose of me. I let go and said sorry straight away because I could see in her aura she was really frightened, and I'd gotten sort of scared as well. Anyway, she was mad at me for a week and wouldn't let me even hold her hand for two weeks after that.

It was only a few days after we had gotten back to the holding hands stage that the Lightning Bringer showed up again. Outside the school, on his black motorcycle, just like he'd done six years before. I felt my heart stop when I saw him, as if something from a nightmare had just walked out into the sun. An awful fear suddenly becoming real.

Which it was, because this time he was smiling at Anya. My Anya! And all those electric tendrils were reaching out for her, blue-spark octopus tentacles, wrapping around and caressing her like I wanted to do but didn't know how.

I tried to hold her back, but she ignored me, and I felt these shivers going through her, like when a dog's fur ripples when you scratch in exactly the right place. Then she pulled her hand out of mine and pushed me away, and I saw her looking at the Lightning Bringer just like Carol had six years before, with her mouth slightly open and her tongue just whisking around to leave her lips wet and her chest pushed forward so the buttons went tight. . . .

I screamed and charged at the man, but he just laughed, and the blue energy came gushing out with his laughter, smacking into me like a fist, and I went down, winded. He laughed again, beating me with power, so all I could do was crawl away and vomit by the bushes next to the gate. Vomit till there was nothing to come up except black bile that choked and burned till it felt like it was taking the skin off the inside of my mouth and nose.

When I finally got up, the Lightning Bringer and Anya were gone. For a second I thought maybe she'd gone home, but I knew she hadn't. She didn't stand a chance. If the Lightning Bringer wanted her, he'd take her. And he'd do whatever he wanted with her, till he got tired, and then she'd be just like Carol. An accidental-death-by-lightning statistic.

I think it was then that I realized that I didn't just like Anya, I was in love with her. I'd been petrified of the

Lightning Bringer for six years, terrified of what he could do, and of the darker fear that I might somehow be like him.

Now all I cared about was Anya and how to get her back, back safe before the thunderclouds in the distance rolled over the town and up the mountain. Because I knew that's where the Lightning Bringer had gone. I felt it, deep inside. He'd gone to get closer to the clouds, and he'd gone to call a storm. It was answering him, the charge building up in the sky, answering the great swell of current in the earth. Soon they would come together.

I think it was about this time that I completely flipped out. Totally crazy. Anyway, the Darly twins later said they saw me running along the mountain road without my shirt, bleeding from scratches all over and frothing at the mouth. I think they made up the frothing, though the scratches were certainly true.

Basically, I turned into a sort of beast, just following the one sense that could lead me to Anya. I could tell where she'd gone from the traces of her apricot aura, and the blue flashes left by the Lightning Bringer. They were intermingled too, and in some deep recess of my mind I knew that they were kissing and those tree-strong hands were roaming over her, her own clasped tightly around him as they'd never been properly clasped around me.

I think it was that thought that started the animal part of me howling . . . but I stopped soon enough, because I needed the breath, just as the first thunderheads rolled above me with the snap of cold air and a few fat drops of rain, the lightning coming swift and terrible behind.

I ran even faster, pain stitching up my side, eating into my lungs, and then I was staggering out onto the lookout parking area and there was the black motorcycle silhouetted against the lightning-soaked sky. I looked around desperately, practically sniffing the aura traces on the ground. Then I saw them, the Lightning Bringer pressing his black-clad body against Anya, her back on the granite stone that marked some local hero's past. She was naked, school dress blown to the storm winds, lips fastened hungrily to the man, arms clasped behind his head. I watched, frozen, as those arms sank lower, hands unzipping his leather trousers, fingers laced behind muscular buttocks.

He raised her legs around him, then thrust forward, his hands reaching toward the sky. With my strange sight I saw streamers fly up from his outstretched fingers, streamers desperately trying to connect with the electric feelers that came questing down from the sky. When they did connect, a million volts would come coursing down through the man's upraised arms—and through Anya.

I ran forward then, leaping onto the Lightning Bringer's back, lifting my hands above his, making the streamers he'd cast my own. He stumbled, and Anya fell away from him, rolling partly down the hill.

Then the lightning struck. In one split, incandescent second it filled me with pure light, charging me with power, too much power to contain, power that demanded a release. It was an ache of pleasure withheld, the moment before orgasm magnified a thousand times. It had to be released before the pleasure burned all my senses away. Suddenly I knew what the Lightning Bringer knew, knew how I could have not only the Power, but the ecstasy of letting part of it run through me to burn its way, uncaring, as I took my pleasure.

"You see!" he crowed, crouching before me, shielding his eyes from the blazing inferno that my aura had become. "You see! Take her, spend the Power! Feed her to the Power!"

I looked down at Anya, seeing her naked for the first time, her pale skin stark against the black tar of the parking area. She was frightened now, partly free from the Lightning Bringer's compulsion.

I started toward her and she screamed, face crumpling. And somewhere in the midst of all the burning, flowing power I remembered her fear—and something else, too.

"I love her," I said to the Lightning Bringer. Then I kissed him right in the middle of his forehead.

I don't know what happened next because I was knocked unconscious. Anya says that both of us turned into one enormous blue-hot ball of chain lightning that bounced backward and forward all across the parking area, burning off her fringe and melting both the motorcycle and the bronze plaque on the stone. It didn't leave anything at all of the Lightning Bringer.

When I came to, I was a bit disoriented because I had my head in Anya's lap and I was looking up at her—but since all her hair was gone, I didn't know who she was for a couple of seconds. She had her dress back on again too, or what was left of her dress. It had some really interesting tears, but I was in no state to appreciate them.

"You'd better go," I croaked up at her, my voice sounding horribly like the Lightning Bringer's. "He might be back."

"I don't think so," she said, rocking me backward and forward like I needed to be soothed or something. I liked it, anyway.

"I'm just like him," I whispered, remembering when I wouldn't stop kissing her, remembering the feel of the Power, wanting to use it to make myself irresistible, to slake its lust and my own on her, make her just a receptacle for pleasure. . . .

"No, you're not," she said, smiling. "You always gave me the choice."

I thought about that for a second, while the dancing black spots in front of my eyes started to fade out and the ringing in my ears quieted down to something like school bells.

"Anya . . . can you see auras?" I said.

"Sometimes, with people I know well," she whispered, bending down to kiss me on the eyes, her breast brushing my ear.

"What color's mine?" I asked. It seemed very important to know, all of a sudden. "It's not blue and kind of . . . kind of . . . electric, is it?"

"No!" she answered firmly, bending over to kiss me properly on the lips. "It's orange, shot with gold. It looks a lot like marmalade."

about "Lightning Bringer"

I have always been interested in lightning. Electrical storms fascinate me, and I love to watch them rolling in, lightning forking down under a sky that is entirely black with thunderheads.

I was almost struck by lightning once. I went out the back door of the house during a storm to put out the trash. Just as I stepped outside, lightning struck the metal drainpipe about twelve feet away. I fell back inside the doorway, momentarily deafened, stunned, and blind. For a few seconds I thought I had actually been struck by lightning. Then my sight and hearing came back and I realized it was only a near miss.

This added a certain personal involvement to my interest in lightning. I felt like I'd somewhat made the acquaintance of an actual lightning bolt. I'd moved up from being in the audience of a storm to becoming a caller at the theater door. That's as close as I care to get. People do survive lightning strikes, but I don't want to try my luck. I can still remember those seconds of blind, deaf, dumbstruck fear.

Given my interest in lightning, I was held spellbound by a television documentary on lightning that aired a few weeks before I wrote "Lightning Bringer". In this documentary they had tremendous specially shot film that showed the "streamers" that flow up from anything vertical. These streamers actually make the connection with the electrical potential held in the storm. I saw ghostly streamers rising up from trees and buildings, from weathercocks, and most importantly, from people.

These upwardly rising streamers are the first part of a lightning strike, so in a way lightning starts from the ground. The taller and stronger the streamer, the more likely that it will connect with the storm. When it does, there is an electrical discharge down from the storm to the ground through the conductor. If the conductor is a metal lightning rod, that's okay. But people are not so well equipped

Garth Nix

to deal with bolts of energy that at their core are as hot as the surface of the Sun.

I vaguely knew how lightning worked, but it wasn't until I saw these strange, luminous streamers rising up out of vertical structures that it really made sense. At the same time, I was struck with the way the streamers varied, even between people of the same height. Some people just had stronger streamers.

I also knew that there were people who tended to get struck by lightning quite a lot, but who still survived. I had a dim memory of a man who was struck by lightning seven times over quite a few years. He was apparently going to the post office to mail the proof of his many lightning strikes to the *Guinness Book of Records* when he was hit by an eighth lightning bolt. He survived that as well, though his clothes were burned off and some of the papers were singed.

Put together, all this gave me the idea for people who could see the streamers and manipulate electrical energy in various ways. Small, secret ways, like controlling the electrical energy in people's minds, or in big, flashy ways, like calling down lightning. That was the central idea. Then I had to find a story to use that idea.

I can never be sure where every part of my actual stories or plots comes from. I don't know why I had a boy with the power to see auras and absorb lightning, or why I had a dangerous drifter with similar powers. I can see where the basic *ideas* come from for most of my stories and books, but I never know how they become stories.

So I can't tell you that. But I can tell you something that might be even more useful. If you're ever caught out in the open during a fierce thunderstorm, with lightning all around, the experts say that the best thing to do is to crouch down into a tight ball with your head tucked in as well. Make yourself as small as possible, because that way the streamer that rises out of you will be lower than any others around, and the lightning won't connect with *you*.

If you like to watch lightning like I do, do it from inside, with a window safely between you and the storm. And never, ever take out the trash when there is thunder roaring overhead.

about Garth Nix

Garth Nix is an Australian author of fantasy and science fiction novels, including *Sabriel* and *Shade's Children,* both of which have won awards in Australia and the U.S. His latest book is *Lirael,* a sequel to *Sabriel.* His highly inventive stories, set in persuasive, complex worlds, are popular with both adults and young adults—*Sabriel* and *Shade's Children* were selected as American Library Association Best Books for Young Adults. Though principally a writer, he continues to work as a part-time literary agent as well.

Garth Nix lives in Sydney, Australia.

He is so homely,
so downright ugly,
that none of the girls
even think about him.

. . . .

So something must be
very wrong with me,
because I want to kiss him.
I want to kiss him real bad.

Secret Shelf

by Sonya Sones

I Am Born

I cry out.
Something is pressed to my lips.
I know what to do.
I suck.
I arch my back
and suck with all
seven pounds six ounces of my strength.
I suck
because my life depends on it,
suck
because I don't know
how to do anything else,
suck
to feel the warm nectar
flowing through me,
filling me up to the tips of my ecstatic toes.

And then I drift,
sated,
off to sleep
and dream
of sucking.

Secret Shelf

Joe

I never should have told Colette
how cute I thought he was.
I never should have pointed out
his hands,
or how he stands
with one foot propped against the wall.
I never should have told her
how I love his lower lip,
or the way I nearly flip
when he walks by me in the hall
and says hello.

I never should have mentioned Joe.

If I had never told Colette
how much I like his lashes
and the silver light
that flashes in his violet eyes,
then she might not have noticed them
and she might not have smiled at him
and he might not have noticed her
and he might not have said hello
or asked her out
or given her his ring,
or anything.

I never should have mentioned Joe.

Sonya Sones

Rain

I used
to love
the rain—

the way it scented the air
with the rich smell of earth,
the way it turned the inside of the car
into a snug cocoon,
the way it painted the streets
with glistening neon light.

Now
I hate the rain.
I hate it for reminding me
of last August on the Vineyard,
when the soft rain licked at my lashes
while your lips covered mine.

I used to love the rain.
You used to love
me.

In My Dreams

I'm dreaming of him kissing me,
of his lips sizzling
all the cells in my body,
of wishing he would remove
every stitch of my clothes.

I'm dreaming of him smiling
a mind reader's smile
and slowly unbuttoning my blouse,
the hundreds and hundreds and hundreds
of buttons on my blouse.

I'm dreaming of my nipples rising up,
yearning to know
how his hands will feel
when he cups his palms
over the lace of my bra.

But just as the last button is undone
and he reaches out to do
what my eyes are commanding him to do,
there's suddenly this invisible force field
between us,

Sonya Sones

and his palms go flat and white against it,
as if he's a mime.
He looks shocked for a second,
then shrugs with an accepting grin
as my alarm wakes me.

Now I'm lying here,
breathless,
thinking that I ought to
at least be able to have him
in my dreams.

Murphy

He is so homely,
so downright ugly,
that none of the girls
even think about him.

He's too lowly,
too pitiful
to even bother
making fun of.

So something must be
very wrong with me,
because I want to kiss him.
I want to kiss him real bad,

even though his nose is crooked
and his ears are huge,
even though his hair's a mess
and his lips are tight and scared.

I want to kiss away
those circles under his eyes
that make him look like
he's never slept a second in his life.

And those scrawny arms of his
seem like they're just aching

Sonya Sones

to hold on to someone.
I wish I could let them hold on to me.

When no one was looking,
I'd walk up to him
and say, "Hey, Murph.
Would it be okay if I kissed you?"

And he'd look hurt
because he'd think I was joking,
and he'd turn away
to hide his face,

but I'd touch his shoulder
and look at him with gentle misty movie eyes
and say, "Come on. I mean it.
I really want to."

And he'd look dumbstruck,
and all the gray
would fade out of his eyes
and this light would come into them

and his lips would look
like they were getting ready to smile
and then, before I had a chance to change my mind,
I'd kiss him,

Secret Shelf

and he'd wrap his skinniness around me
and his arms would be shaking,
and suddenly I'd feel all this love,
all this need pouring into me

right through his lips
into me
and it would feel great,
and I'd close my eyes to feel it better.

And when we stopped to catch our breath,
and I opened them again,
I'd notice this one dark curl
hanging down in the middle of his forehead

and I'd think
how sexy it looked
and wonder why
I'd never noticed it before.

Sonya Sones

The Mockingbird

I'm watching him up there,
silhouetted on the wire,
alone against
the silky blue sky,
belting out the songs
that he's borrowed
from all the other birds,

trying on
one voice after another,
pausing briefly
between each one
to see if he's attracting
the girl bird
of his dreams,

and every now and then
he dances up into the air,
fluttering in a loop
that shows off the patches of white
etched on his wings,
before landing back down on the wire
to begin another song.

And as I watch him,
I'm feeling a lot like him,
like a feathery creature

balancing on a wire,
trying on lots of different voices
to see which one
works best

and every now and then,
doing a little twirl
out on the dance floor,
hoping the boy bird of my dreams
will fly by and notice me,
flutter down beside me
and ask me to dance.

Sonya Sones

Looking Out

I'm sleeping over
at Sarah's tonight,
at her father's place
on the sixteenth floor of Shawnessy Suites.
Sarah's taking a bath,
and her father and I
are watching Wheel of Fortune.

He seems so much younger,
so much cooler
than my father,
sitting here next to me
on the couch,
sipping a glass of champagne,
cracking jokes about Vanna.

When a commercial comes on,
he picks up a pair of binoculars
and walks over to the wall of glass
to look into the windows
of the surrounding apartments.
And I can't help wondering
what he's seeing.

He glances over at me and grins,
then asks me if I'd like to take a peek.
I hesitate, but he says,

"Aw, come on. It's much more fun than TV."
So I take the binoculars
and scan the rows of windows,
surprised by how close they seem.

I can see a man shaking his finger
at a girl with spiked blue hair,
a somber woman playing the cello
in her nightgown,
a cat staring intently at a huge aquarium,
an old man flexing his muscles
in front of a mirror,

and two stories up
and one window over,
a woman is looking out
at the night,
and now a man with no shirt
is coming up behind her,
wrapping his arms around her

and suddenly I feel his arms
wrapping around me
only it isn't the man with no shirt
it's Sarah's father
and his hot lips are kissing my neck
and an awful shudder is racing through me
and I'm shoving him away

Sonya Sones

and a second later
Sarah comes through the door and says,
"Oh. I love Daddy's binos. Can I have a turn?"
And while she's looking through them,
her father grabs hold of my wrist and
puts one finger up to his lips,
warning me not to tell.

I'm sleeping over
at Sarah's tonight,
at her father's place
on the sixteenth floor of Shawnessy Suites,
but I never
will
again.

Secret Shelf

I'm rifling through the dust and jumble
of my parents' walk-in closet,
searching for the perfect belt
to wear with my new blue skirt,

when I happen to glance up
and see a small shelf
above the door
crammed with paperback books.

Strange to think that
I've been in this closet
hundreds of times before
and never once noticed it till now.

I pull over the chair
from my mother's dressing table,
climb up to take a closer look,
and just about faint:

here are some of
the dirtiest books
I've ever seen
in my life.

I try to picture
my mother and father

Sonya Sones

sitting around reading them,
but it's just too gross

and I suddenly realize
that I'll never be able
to think of my parents
in quite the same way as I used to

and that every time they go out
and leave me alone in the house,
I'll be racing right back up here
to grab another one off the shelf.

Secret Shelf

Why I Bother with Algebra

One day
I'll be walking
down the street
and a frantic
but very handsome guy
will rush up to me
and say, "Excuse me,
but I don't suppose
you happen to know
the discriminant of
$2x$ squared $- 3x + 5$?
It's really important!"
And I'll smile sweetly
and say,
"Why, of course I do.
It's seven."
He'll say,
"Oh, thank you, thank you!
You don't know how much
this means to me!
I've got to go now,
but
could I have
your phone number?"

Sonya Sones

The Ride Home

After Zak's party,
Rachel's big sister
came to drive a bunch of us home,
with her friend
and her friend's younger brother.

I was the last one to get in the car,
and it turned out
all the other laps were taken,
so I had to sit on
Rachel's sister's friend's brother's lap.

I'd never seen him before,
but he had such smoldery dark eyes
that I felt like I'd been zapped
smack into the middle
of some R-rated movie

and everyone else in the car
was just going to fade away
and this guy and I were going to start making out,
right then and there,
without ever having said one word to each other.

But what really happened
was that he blushed and said, "Hi. I'm Dylan."
And I blushed back and said, "I'm Sophie."

And he said, "Nice name."
And I said, "Thanks."

After that we didn't say anything else,
but our bodies seemed to be
carrying on a conversation of their own,
leaning together into every curve of the road,
sharing skin secrets.

And just before we got to my house,
I thought I felt him
give my waist an almost squeeze.
Then the car rolled to a stop and I climbed out
with my whole body buzzing.

I said good night,
headed up the front walk,
and when I heard the car pulling away,
I looked back over my shoulder
and saw Dylan looking over his shoulder at me.

When our eyes connected,
this miracle smile
lit up his face
and I practically had
a religious experience.

Sonya Sones

Then I went upstairs to bed
and tried to fall asleep,
but I felt permanently wide awake.
And every time I closed my eyes,
I saw that smile and felt that almost squeeze.

Daydream

I can almost taste
the shivery wind
rosing my cheeks,

almost smell the soft scents
of pine needle
and new snow,

almost see the misted strands of sun
streaking the drifts
on the forest floor,

almost hear the water gurgling
under the frozen surface
of the pond,

almost feel the mirror-smooth ice
gliding past
beneath my skates

and the warmth
of your gloved hand
holding mine . . .

Sonya Sones

Between Classes with Dylan

We fall into step
in the crowded hall
without even glancing
at each other,

but his little finger
finds mine,
hooking us
together,

and all the clatter
of the corridor fades away,
till the only sound I can hear
is the whispering of our fingers.

I Wish

I wish I could drink a magic potion and

shrink way down till I was small

enough to fit right into his

shirt pocket and live

there tucked near to

his heart listening

to it beating in

rhythm with

mine every

minute of

every

day

Sonya Sones

Hair Prayer

His hand's
in my hair.
May he leave it
right there
until April
or May,
near the nape
of my neck
just below
my left ear.
Let it stay
where it is,
right here
in my hair
and not go
anywhere
for a year
and a day.
Better yet,
let it stay
till I'm gray.

about "Secret Shelf"

People often talk about having an inner child, but I have an inner teenager. And like most teenagers, my inner teen is obsessed with sex. So she was very helpful when I was writing the poems for this anthology. In fact, she would probably argue that she wrote them by herself, without any help from me. And you might even believe her. She can be very persuasive. Last week she almost had me convinced I should get my bellybutton pierced. Which is *not* a good look for someone my age.

One of the reasons it's so easy for me to get in touch with my inner teen, is that I've been keeping diaries and journals since I was old enough to be a cheerleader. I have boxes and boxes of them stored away in my closet. And often, when I'm trying to remember what it was like in the bad old days, I leaf through them. And it's all there. Every miserable moment.

Most of the poems included here are from my forthcoming book, *What My Mother Doesn't Know.* It's a novel written in poetry, that tells the story of Sophie, a fourteen-and-a-half-year-old girl who's trying to figure out the difference between love and lust. Although I'm considerably older than Sophie, I'm not at all sure I've figured out the difference yet myself.

My first book, *Stop Pretending,* is autobiographical. It tells the story of what happened on the eve of my thirteenth birthday, when my older sister had a nervous breakdown and had to be hospitalized. Toward the end of that book, which is also written in poetry, there are some poems about my first love, a boy named John. I had such a good time writing about those first feelings of overwhelming passion, that I knew I wanted to delve into them more deeply. That's when the poems for *What My Mother Doesn't Know* began bubbling to the surface.

Unlike the poems in *Stop Pretending,* these poems are definitely *not* autobiographical. Especially not the embarrassing ones. I made all the embarrassing ones up. Every single one of them. Just ask my inner teen.

about Sonya Sones

Sonya Sones has worked as a film animator, a script supervisor, a still photographer, and a film editor. Her interest in writing led her to enroll in a UCLA poetry class taught by Myra Cohn Livingston, who set her on the path to writing her acclaimed first book, *Stop Pretending: What Happened When My Big Sister Went Crazy.* That novel in verse was a finalist for the *Los Angeles Times* Book Prize and the winner of a Christopher Award, the Claudia Lewis Poetry Award, and the Myra Cohn Livingston Award for Poetry. It was also an American Library Association Best Book for Young Adults and a Top Ten Quick Pick for Reluctant Young Adult Readers.

Sonya Sones lives near the beach in California with her family and her fifty rose bushes.

And then I see it. I'm drawn to it, pulled toward it, my feet change direction without telling me why.

A snake. A beautiful, nasty, enchanting snake. A serpent wound around the arms of a tall, skinny woman with white, spiky hair. I've never seen anything like it. The snake is almost orange, a pale orange, with yellow sun splotches along its back and tiny red eyes.

"Can I touch it?" I ask the woman.

Snake

by Laurie Halse Anderson

I'm not going on a date, I'm walking into the fires of hell. I have to spend the day with the daughter of my father's boss. A blind date with Lily Covington. You can't even call it a date, really; it's punishment, torture, slow death by the sea. Shit.

"This means a lot to me, son," Dad says. "Anything we can do to keep the Covingtons happy will help."

He gives me the once-over. I'm wearing a blue polo shirt, khakis, and a pair of cheap brown shoes he bought, a size too small. I look harmless, like the guy who takes you to your booth at Friendly's. Dad grunts. I pass inspection.

My dad is Bob Willard, a California Carpet King, master of berber and plush pile. He has devoted his life to carpets. He sells it by the mile, roll after roll of itchy, fuzzy, chemical-laden carpet. He sells it 365 days a year, and it keeps a roof over our heads, clothes on our backs, and food in our mouths. (He reminds me of this from time to time.) And now the Big Boss, G. D. Covington IV himself, owner of the entire Carpet King chain, is in town. Dad's sucking up big time. He wants a promotion. Regional manager. We need the money. So I'm getting ready for the date from hell.

I reach down and loosen the laces on the shoes. I was supposed to be surfing today, the first time in weeks. Another month and I'll be in college—well, community college. Between that and work I'll probably never see the ocean again. I wiggle my toes. I'm going to have blisters by the end of the day. Shit.

My father, G. D. Covington IV, is an idiot. No, not just an idiot, he's a moron, an imbecile, a fool. It's July and I'm on vacation. Am I on the beach? No. Am I hanging out with friends? No. I am three thousand miles away from home. Daddy decided we needed to bond. Daddy decided to drag me on a seven-city tour of his nasty carpet showrooms. And when he got tired of me pouting, Daddy decided I needed a date.

Daddy is going to regret this.

I can't take her to Paramount Studios, or the Hollywood sign, or Sunset Boulevard, or Warner Brothers—nothing that normal girls want to do when they come to Los Angeles. According to my father, Lily Covington is a brain, a pretty brain, a pretty, sweet, virgin brain who is not interested in the movies, television, or other normal things. We're going to the art museum, then lunch, and then something really intense, like a doll show, until our dads are finished with their meeting and I can dump her.

Seven cities, seven lame dates. If he's another Date #3, Kansas City, I'll use my pepper spray. Kansas City acted like he

Laurie Halse Anderson

was an altar boy until we were alone, then he turned into a WWF takedown specialist. Nobody takes down Lily Covington—not without my permission.

"Lily!" Daddy roars from the other end of the hotel suite.

"Coming," I call. Quick mirror check: skirt (not too short), shirt with three-quarter-length sleeves, chunky shoes, stockings, hair in a ponytail, no makeup. This all according to a memo from Daddy Dearest—honest. He started choosing my outfits after Disaster Date #2, Newark, New Jersey. I was just trying to be the teensiest bit fashionable, and not that I'm trying to brag or anything, but #2 told my father that he thought I was the hottest little piece he had ever seen. It was a very short date.

"Lily!" Dadman the caveman, Neanderthal in a thousand-dollar suit. God, this is so embarrassing. Date the boss's daughter, get a raise. Make her smile and we'll throw in a free crate of Stain-Off.

Dad and Mr. Covington holler at each other like long-lost lovers across the lobby of the Beverly Hills Hotel.

"Bob!"

"G. D.!"

They embrace, pound each other on the back, then release. That's how bullshitters and football players hug. The boss is bigger than my dad and dressed way better. He looks like he works out. When he sees me staring at him, he glares, but pastes on a fake salesman grin.

"So, this is your boy," says Mr. G. D. Covington IV, sizing me up. "Not a slacker, is he?"

"Ho, ho, no," chuckles Dad. "Matter of fact, he spent all of last summer on his knees installing that new three-ply plush at a mansion up in the canyons."

"Learning from the ground up, eh?" Mr. Covington asks.

"Yes, sir," I say as I stick out my hand to shake. "It was quite a summer. On my knees."

"Good," he says, gripping my hand. "I like a lad who's not afraid to work."

No one has ever called me a lad before. Is this exec-speak?

He looks in my eyes, hypnotizing me as he increases the pressure on my hand. "Lily will be down in a minute," G. D. "Death Grip" Covington assures me. He compresses the bones in my hand, mashing tendons, separating knuckles. "She's really looking forward to this."

"I can't wait to meet her," I squeak.

On cue, the elevator doors swish open. He releases me.

Lily has arrived.

Oh, God.

Oh, God.

Not another one. Does Daddy order them from the same place he gets his suits? Preppy pants, a department-store shirt, butt-ugly shoes, and surfer-blond hair. Looks like he's a few french fries short of a Happy Meal, sort of dazed. And why is he holding his hand like that?

"Here's my little girl," *Daddy says as I join them, the Carpet Kings and one young Carpet Prince. I smile at the prince, he smiles backs. Fake, fake, fake. Good, we're both unhappy about this.*

I wink at him just to piss off Daddy. I am arm candy. Lick me. No, not really, no licking. Let's just get this over with.

"Hungry?" I ask as I pull out onto Sunset Boulevard.

Lily shakes her head. She was plenty sweet to me in front of her father, but as soon as we were alone in the car, she flipped a switch and turned off the charm. She's better looking than I expected, kind of short, but built, her clothes what you would expect from the East Coast. For a minute back there in the lobby I thought this would work out. But not anymore.

"Want to see the driveways of the stars?" I try. That usually makes out-of-towners laugh.

Nothing.

I pass a moving van. This is so lame. I should have told him no, flat no, total no. At some point you have to say no to your dad, right? Everybody does it. My dad must have done it to Grandpa. Just no.

Chicken—*bwak!*

I try again. "I got the whole day planned. Matter of fact, it's been planned for a week. I had to e-mail it to your father's secretary and get it approved. Kind of strict, isn't he?"

She stares at the bumper sticker on the rust heap in front of us. NEVER GIVE IN. NEVER, NEVER, NEVER, NEVER.

I hit the turn signal and swerve into the left lane,

Snake

accelerate to make the light, and head for the highway.

"Do you always drive like that?" she asks.

"Like what?"

"Slow down."

Pushy bitch. I tap the brakes as we crest a hill and hit a wall of traffic, six lanes of cars creeping forward. Damn.

"Don't worry," I assure her. "We'll get off at the next exit. I know a shortcut to the museum."

She shakes her head so hard the ponytail swishes. "No museums. If you take me to a museum, I'll stay in the car all day, I swear. Even if I cook to death in the parking garage, I'm not moving."

"Well, at least you're talking," I say. "That's progress. We have to go to the museum. I promised your father."

"What are you, a Boy Scout or something?"

She doesn't mean that in a nice way. I sigh. This day sucks already and my feet are killing me. It's not even noon.

"How about Mann's Chinese Theatre, you know, where all the celebrity handprints are?"

"What do I look like, a tourist?"

I bite my tongue so hard it bleeds. Keep her happy. Just keep her happy. Then it hits me—the perfect thing to do.

"The La Brea Tar Pits!" he shouts.

"You're kidding, right?"

"The Getty?"

"I said no museums."

"Will Rogers Park? The Viper Room? Ed Debevic's? Forest

　　　　　　Laurie Halse Anderson

Lawn Cemetery—*great dead people there.*"

Now I'm worried. I reach in my purse and feel around for my pepper spray. "Do you usually take girls to a cemetery on a first date?"

"This isn't a first date. It's not a date at all." He leans on the horn and honks loudly. So obnoxious.

"That doesn't help," I point out. "We're stuck."

"It makes me feel better."

"Well, it's giving me a headache."

He stops honking. We sit in the car and stew. It smells like sour milk in here. I bet his dad made him clean it out this morning. I wish I had enough guts to open the door and get out, just walk away from him, from this. I'd go . . . I don't know where I'd go. That's the problem.

"Look, what's your name again?" I ask.

"Adam. Adam Willard."

"Okay, Adam Willard. Neither one of us wants to be here, but we don't have a choice. Let's call a truce." I reach out my hand. "Shake?"

He looks at my hand like it's going to bite him. "Truce," he agrees.

The car inches ahead.

"Where are you from?" he asks. "Rochester or something?"

"Buffalo. Buffalo, New York."

Adam pulls into the far lane and we pick up speed. He glances over at me. "Where they get all the snow?"

I nod. It's so depressing to be from a place everyone knows from the Weather Channel.

He grins as he checks the rearview mirror. Now we're moving.
"Then there is only one place to take you."

"Venice Beach," I say, gesturing to the ocean, the sand, and a sea of people flowing around us.

"Cool," she says under her breath.

Venice Beach is where people come to be themselves and other people come to watch. Rollerbladers in bathing suits whiz by the artists, musicians, massage therapists, and sunglass salesmen lining the concrete boardwalk. Incense mixes with the Pacific breeze, a saxophone wails with the screams of little children flying a kite.

We wander the boardwalk. A middle-aged soccer mom gets her belly button pierced. Japanese tourists crowd around a psychic for tarot readings. A heavily tattooed, blue-haired boy, his chest and back a garden of blooming flowers, plays Mozart for quarters. Lily gets off on the gentle weirdness. She buys toe rings and mango juice and has her hands hennaed.

"Is it always like this?" she finally asks as we stop to watch a juggler.

"Always."

The juggler spins faster, keeping two apples, an orange, and a pineapple in the air.

"He's pretty good," Lily says.

The juggler overhears her, and winks. Lily blushes. It makes her prettier.

"This guy's nothing," I say. "There used to be a dude who

juggled chainsaws—running chainsaws."

"Liar. No one juggles chainsaws. Except maybe my father's secretary."

Was that a smile? A hint of a smile? No, just my imagination.

The juggler claps his hands twice and tosses the fruit into the crowd. Lily reaches out and grabs an apple, round and deep red. She holds it out for me to take a bite, then snatches it back at the last minute. I chase her down the boardwalk, cursing under my breath as the blisters on my feet pop, pop, pop. Lily pulls up suddenly.

"Oh, look!" she says with a sharp intake of breath. "Muscles!"

"This is Muscle Beach," Adam explains.

He's wrong. This is heaven. Men, strong beefy men as far as the eye can see, are lifting weights right here on the sand. Some of them are those gross action-figure weirdos with veins sticking out along their neck, but most of them are yummy cover boys. I'm hungry. I step off the boardwalk and mingle with the muscles. Adam is close behind me.

"They say this all started back in the thirties."

Right, blah, blah, blah. He gives a history lesson I don't hear. I join a crowd watching a Greek god raise a barbell above his head. All the women and about half the men in the audience are admiring the guy's, ahem, equipment. Those Speedos don't leave much to the imagination, thank goodness.

He sets the barbell in the sand and struts over to a chin-up bar. He jumps up and grabs the bar, then lets go with one hand and does five perfect one-handed chin-ups. I didn't even know that was possible. Now, why couldn't Daddy have set me up with someone like that?

Adam crosses his arms over his chest. "Big deal," he mutters.

"Oh, yeah? I'd like to see you do that."

"Dressed like this? No way," he says. "Besides, he's probably gay."

I'll never understand the way guys think.

"What does that have to do with anything?" I ask. "He's buff, he's gorgeous, and it doesn't matter if he's gay or not." Though secretly I really hope he's not, because that would just wreck this fantasy I'm starting to have.

The crowd moves off and follows the one-handed chin-up hunk. Adam steps in front of me.

"Come on, I got other stuff to show you," he says.

"I want to look around. We don't have anything like this in Buffalo." My fantasy man has disappeared into the crowd.

Adam leaps up and grabs the chin-up bar. "I won't pretend I can do it with one hand," he says as he strains his way through a set of sloppy chin-ups. "One . . . two . . . three . . . four. But this is cake. Eight . . . nine."

His form is terrible. He's not even dipping all the way down. Should I do it? It doesn't seem fair. But I hate this macho crap.

Adam half finishes the last chin-up, releases the bar, and drops to the sand, his face red and sweaty. "Ten!" he crows.

I reach down and unbuckle my shoes. "Boost me up," I say. "I want to try."

Laurie Halse Anderson

"You can't do chin-ups," he says.

"You did," I point out. "Boost me up."

Adam rolls his eyes. "All right." He places his hands around my waist, warm hands. "One, two"—I bend my legs a little—"three!"

I leap, he lifts, and I grab the bar.

"Don't worry if you fall," Adam says. "I'll catch you."

"What'll you give me if I can do a chin-up?" I ask, hanging in midair.

"I'll buy you ice cream."

"And if I can do ten?"

He laughs. "Anything you want, Lily. Anything you want."

A couple of people have drifted over to watch. They think they see a spoiled sixteen-year-old white girl from Buffalo in way over her head. Ha! I move my hands a bit, then start to pull. One chin-up, two, three. Piece of cake. Four, five, six. Nice and smooth. The muscles in my arms, my shoulders, my back, all contract rhythmically. Seven, eight, nine, ten, eleven. I'm stoked. No wonder these guys like working out on the beach. The breeze is clean, the ocean rolls in forever, and with all these people around, it's like a party. Twelve, thirteen, fourteen, fifteen. Arms getting hot. Sixteen, seventeen. Slowing down, concentrate, Lil, show him. Eighteen. Someone in the crowd claps and cheers me on. It's not Adam. Nineteen. One more. My palms slip a little. I know I look dumb, but this feels really good. Pull, pull, pull—twenty!

I release the bar and drop to the sand. A few people clap. I curtsy. Damn, I'm good.

"Gymnastics," she says. "I placed third in the state last year. Whew, it's hot." She starts to unbutton her shirt.

"Stop!" I shout. "You can't do that—this isn't a nude beach." I clutch the front of her shirt to hold it closed. I am having simultaneous thoughts, evidence of a brain fried from standing in the sun:

1. She looked really hot doing chin-ups.
2. She just kicked my ass doing chin-ups.
3. Her breasts are small, but very close to my fingertips.
4. I have a wicked boner.

This day is not going as planned.

Lily peels my hands off. "It's linen," she says. "It wrinkles. And my sport bra covers up more than these so-called bathing suits."

She takes off her blouse and ties it around her waist, then, in a flash, strips off her panty hose and throws them in the garbage. Somehow I don't think her father's secretary would approve.

She pulls the rubber-band-thing out of her ponytail and her hair escapes, a gold curtain. It changes her whole face, having her hair down. Having her shirt off changes a few things, too. I pull my shirt off over my head. Don't want her to feel out of place or anything.

Lily studies me. "Stop sucking in your gut," she says. "You look fine. Sort of hot, even."

I guess that's what passes for a compliment in Buffalo.

"Hang on." I pull off my stupid shoes and socks and toss them in the trash barrel.

"You're throwing out your shoes?"

"My father bought them for me. They're too small."

I curl my toes in the sand. Happy toes, happy naked feet.

A filthy guy pushing a shopping cart takes my shoes out of the trash. He looks them over, nods to me once, sets them carefully in the cart, and pushes off. Lily watches, eyes wide.

"Is he homeless?" she whispers.

"I don't know. At least he's not shoeless."

We walk back up to the boardwalk. The breeze picks up Lily's hair and plays with it.

"I should have warned him," I say. "Those are magic shoes. If he puts them on, he could be transformed into Bob Willard's son and have to live out my life."

Lily laughs. "Good thing he didn't take my panty hose."

A cell phone rings. People standing around us all check to see if the call is for them.

"It's me," Lily says, pulling a sleek silver phone from her purse. "Hello?"

More excuses. Daddy's meeting is running late, important business, yada, yada, yada. He tells me that no, we won't be going out to dinner like he promised, and no, we won't be going to the movie premiere like he promised. For a second I think about crying. But only for a second. Mostly I feel tired, sunburned, foreign. I drop the phone in the sand and watch it talk. If I buried it and came back in a hundred years to dig it up, I bet

Daddy would still be saying the same things.

I pick up the phone and say good-bye to my father's voice.

"What's up?" Adam asks.

"Change of plans. You can just drop me off at the hotel. I'm going to order room service and watch Buffy.*" I start walking in the direction of the car.*

"Wait," Adam says. "I thought you had big plans for tonight."

"G. D. Covington IV has big plans for tonight. Not me. I don't want to talk about it. Can we go?"

Adam looks at me, really looks at me—Lily—not some boob who wasted his day, or just a girl, or whatever. But I'm headed back to Buffalo tomorrow, so I'm not really going to look at him, to see what's under the Carpet Prince.

"Okay, let's go."

We walk without talking, past the coffee shop, past the bongo players and a sign that says "HUGS, $2." They are setting up to film a commercial on the beach, probably want to catch the sun going down.

And then I see it. I'm drawn to it, pulled toward it, my feet change direction without telling me why.

A snake. A beautiful, nasty, enchanting snake. A serpent wound around the arms of a tall, skinny woman with white, spiky hair. I've never seen anything like it. The snake is almost orange, a pale orange, with yellow sun splotches along its back and tiny red eyes.

"Can I touch it?" I ask the woman.

"It's a her."

"Can I touch her?"

"You're not scared?" Adam asks.

"Not of this," I say.

"Five bucks," the woman says.

"What?"

Adam looks embarrassed. "It costs five dollars to hold the snake. This is California."

"For ten you get a color photo," the woman says.

"I just want to hold her," I say.

Adam pulls out his wallet and hands the woman a five. The snake does not look at the money. She watches me.

The woman pockets the bill and takes her pet-friend-toy off like she is a jacket or a cape. She tells me not to move and not to scream, then settles the weight of the warm orange snake around my shoulders and arms.

Oooooooohhhh.

Soft and warm, heavy, much heavier than I thought. She slithers across my skin, deliciously alive. How stupid is this, that I'm falling in love with a snake, "an albino Burmese python, ten feet long, at least fifty pounds," the skinny woman tells Adam. But it's not stupid, it's just there. And it's not the snake so much, it's how I feel. Lightning crackles under my skin. Adam feels it too. He's seeing me again, and I can't help it, but I'm seeing him, the boy, the almost man with blistered feet, surfer hair, and a killer smile.

The snake coils her head loosely around my wrist and turns back to look at me, her tongue flicking to take my temperature, test my mood.

"You look good in a snake," Adam says.

*My muscles ripple under the muscles of the python. "Touch
her," I say.*

I reach out and put my hand on Lily's shoulder. Her skin
is warm, hot even, and smooth as water. My hand follows
the curve of her neck to the base of her head, where her hair
drapes over the snake, the same color, the same pattern of
yellow, gold, sunset orange. She raises her hand, the snake
wrapped around it like a bracelet. I take her fingertips, turn
the hand over, and kiss her palm gently. The snake's tongue
flicks, whipping my cheek.

"Thank you," Lily says.

I don't know who she's talking to: me, the snake, the
woman, or someone else.

"Next customer," the snake handler says as she lifts the
python off Lily. I'm still holding her hand. I don't know how
to let go of it. We walk west, down the beach, into the ocean
without a word.

The water rolls in around our waists. It lifts Lily up off
her feet and she giggles. The snake cracked her brittle sugar
shell, and the water washes it away, all the anger about her
dad, her questions. It has softened her tongue, brightened
her eyes. The water is magic.

I'm going to kiss her. I need to know what she tastes like,
if she's salty or sweet. I want to hold her body against mine,
warm and wet, slippery delight. A wave pushes me toward
her. The sunset has turned her eyes tropical green, with
flashes of amber in them. Damn. How did she catch me

　　　　　　　Laurie Halse Anderson

when I wasn't looking?

I'm going to kiss her. You can tell when a girl wants to be kissed.

I hope.

If I don't kiss him soon, I'll explode. I don't even like him—he's a rent-a-date, he's all wrong for me, and it's not like this relationship has a hope in hell. I shiver. I'm boiling. God, I want him. Just a kiss. His lips look soft, his hands are strong.

The water swells underneath me and I pull close to him. He smells like salt, his salt, sea salt, me salt. The sun rolls toward the water behind him. When it hits, it's going to sizzle.

I put my hands on his face and bring him in to me.

about "Snake"

Growing up in the Northeast (Syracuse, New York), I always had an image of California as being this slightly wild, dangerous place. When I first visited it a few years ago, I knew I was right. There is a freedom on the West Coast, an openness to explore identity and sexuality that is not found anywhere else. With freedom come risks, but that's another story. For me, California is the Garden of Eden before God got pissed, a paradise of eternal adolescence.

The names in this story are, of course, deliberate. I based Lily on Lilith, who, according to some religious texts, was Adam's first wife. She was equal to him and took off when he tried to rule over her.

Adam and Lily are caught between leaving childhood and coming into their own as adults. Forced together by their fathers, they start out bitter and end up in each other's arms. Love is like that sometimes.

I think every teenage couple goes through a magic moment of discovery, of feeling like they are the only two people on the planet. I wanted this story to build up to that moment. I remember mine very well. It was a different situation, but just as delicious.

Laurie Halse Anderson

about Laurie Halse Anderson

Laurie Halse Anderson's first young adult novel, *Speak*, was a Michael L. Printz Honor Book and a finalist for the National Book Award and the *Los Angeles Times* Book Prize—an amazing success, by any measure. Her second novel, *Fever 1793*, a historical thriller, made the New York Public Library's 100 Best Books of 2000. She is also the author of a middle-grade series called Wild at Heart, several picture books, and a nonfiction parenting book.

Laurie Halse Anderson, who lives in Pennsylvania, has two daughters, a husband, and way too many books.

He hits the floor, crawls on his belly like in a scene from Guadalcanal, until he reaches his bed, reaches under his bed, reaches his collection.

He pulls out one magazine. No, not that one, the other one. Yes. And that one, that one, that one.

They are spread out on the floor in front of him, and he is spread out on the floor in front of them.

He is investigating the scenes. His beloved scenes. The girl scenes, the girl-girl scenes. The guy-girl scenes. The guy scenes.

He is investigating himself, assessing himself, bits of himself pressed against the carpeted floor.

The Cure for Curtis

by Chris Lynch

"You could come over now, I guess," Curtis says.

"Ya," Lisa answers lazily, "I could, I guess. Or you could come over here."

"Ya," he says, and the line goes all but dead between them.

On her bed, in her shorty Baltimore Orioles nightie, Lisa is paying a fair bit more attention to the drama on her television than to the one in her personal life.

"Could you turn that down?" Curtis asks. "It's kind of screechy, y'know?"

On his bed, in his boxer briefs, Curtis couldn't care much less whether Lisa was listening to him or to Leonardo DiCaprio squealing his way through Shakespeare.

Lisa turns the sound down one tick. It doesn't make jack of a difference, but it passes for cooperation.

"How's that?" she says.

"Great," he says. "Thanks. So, I guess I'll let you go, then."

"Okay, then, I guess I'll let you go. Call me tomorrow night. Don't forget."

"I will. I won't."

Curtis and Lisa make kissing noises into the phone in lieu of saying good-bye.

Curtis flops over the side of his bed and looks underneath. Upside down, with his long black hair sweeping the carpet, he browses his modest library of soft to medium-core pornography.

Image upon image, man upon woman. Upon woman. Upon man. Curtis swims in a sea of bodies, Caligula's own pool of flesh. Wriggling, there has never been such wriggling, like a can of giant-size fishing worms with arms faces hands feet nipples tongues penises. Giant, giant. Slick and wet. Men on women on men. Women. Women on women on women. On Leonardo DiCaprio. On Lisa. Thin and sleek and weightless, every last lost body, nowhere to go but up. And down. Women on men on men on men. On Leonardo. On Curtis. Sweat rolls over every body, sweat becomes orange oil, orange oil lubes everyone into one viscous mass, rubbing and rubbing, rubbing and rubbing until Lisa is rubbed, rubbed away, rubbed out. Rubbing, rubbing, rubbing, rubbing, away, curves away gone. Hard angles, hard muscles, hard hairy, stubble-scraping tongue. Oil, rubbing, warm, cream, hands on it, mouth on it, hands on hips, hips to mouth, hands on it again, hard, wet, front, back, top, bottom, hard, harder, harder. Familiar faces and strange ones, beautiful cut-glass faces and soft, smooth ones emerge out of the soup. The faces come to Curtis. Curtis, the center of it

Chris Lynch

all. Curtis, the slippery, dripping center. Everything comes to Curtis, and Curtis comes to everything.

"Phil. Phil, you have to come over here right now."

"Who is this?"

Phil is Curtis's cousin, his best friend, the older brother he didn't have. Phil knows everything about Curtis and serves as his adviser, confidant, and protector. When Curtis's father, Curtis, died under tragic and mysterious circumstances scuba diving off of Goa when he was supposed to be getting his chemotherapy in Providence, it was Phil who was called in to help the boy get through it. Phil knows the sound of Curtis's *breathing*, never mind the sound of his voice on the telephone.

"Cut it out, Phil. It's me."

"It is? You don't sound like you."

"It's me. And I need you to come over here. And bring a joint."

"I don't have a joint."

"Phil! Phil, man, I am serious. Bring a joint, and come over here now. I have to talk to you."

"Jesus, kid, what did you do?"

"Nothing. I didn't do anything, but I'm gonna. I'm gonna do something awful today, and if you don't come over here and talk me out of it, I swear—"

"All right, all right, but just—can't you come over here, or meet me someplace in between?"

"No. I can't. I can't leave the house, Phil, 'cause I'm

afraid. Petrified I'll do something before I even get there. I'm, like, crazy, totally shithouse over this, so get over here, get over here, get over here."

"I'll get over there, just . . . I gotta get some breakfast, then I'll—"

"Get over here, Phil!"

"Jesus, okay. Is Ma cooking breakfast?"

Ma is not Phil's ma, she is his aunt. They are, however, very close.

"I don't know. I haven't left the room yet. I can't go out."

"Well, smell. You smell fat in the air?"

"Ya, Phil, the air is, like, foggy with fat. Get over here. I need you, man. I really, really need you."

While Curtis waits, he goes back to doing what he has been doing since 4:30 A.M. Lying on his bed, staring at the sheet covering his body, and sweating.

"What is it? You all right? What happened? You in trouble? You sick? What do we have to do?"

Phil is likewise sweating as he comes through the bedroom door. He is wearing copper-colored sweatpants and a blowsy gray Nike "Just Do It" T-shirt. He has a glass of orange juice in one hand and a plate of French toast and link sausages in the other.

"I told her I didn't want anything to eat," Curtis says.

"It's not yours, it's mine." Phil sits on the corner of the bed and stares at his cousin.

Curtis stares back.

"So, what?" Phil asks.

Curtis just continues staring. Then he looks away, out the window at the telephone pole covered in wires and bird shit and hard July sunshine.

"What now, what?" Phil asks again, but with sausage meat muffling his vowels.

Curtis looks to him once more, but little has changed. He still can't speak.

"The hell did you do?" Phil asks, and stops chewing.

Curtis's eyes go all glassy.

Bang bang bang bang.

"Go away, Ma," Phil says.

"What is going on?" Ma asks. "What did he do? Did you find out what he did?"

"No. How am I gonna find out what he did if you won't leave us to it?"

"I didn't do nothin'," Curtis calls, choking up.

A whimper is all that comes from Ma's side of the door.

"You ain't helpin' us out there, Ma."

Silence.

"There," Phil says, resuming eating, "I took care of that for you, didn't I? Don't I always take care of you? Whatever you got this time, I'm sure I can handle it. Why don't you start talkin'."

"Where's the joint?"

"It's nine o'clock in the morning. You don't need no joint."

"Where's the joint, Phil? I can't talk without it. Can't even get out of bed today without it."

Phil is looking down at his plate, sopping up white mud puddles of I Can't Believe It's Not Butter and confectioners' sugar with his French toast. He is in no hurry to produce the joint, as his appetite is quite healthy as it is. He sets the plate down on the bed and takes his juice glass up off the floor.

He is looking out of the corner of his eye at Curtis as he drinks.

"Are you gonna cry, Curt?" Phil says, wiping away pulpy orange bits with the back of his hand.

"I don't think so," Curtis says gently, with a sniff, "but anything's possible."

Phil puts the glass down, removes the fat joint from his sock. Phil lights it and takes his good fair share, three hits in a row, as a matter of fact. It is a shrewd move, because from that point on he doesn't get much.

"Give it over," Phil says after watching Curtis take three, four long hard hits, pause for breath, then take two more. "Give it over, animal."

Curtis finally gives it over but holds on long to the smoke inside him. He lets go slowly as he begins speaking. "I am. An animal. I am, too."

Phil has had little of his own smoke before Curtis crawls out and over the sheet to snatch it back. He remains there, posed like a cat, in boxer briefs, one paw to his lips.

Phil's eyes are wide, and he leans back away, sizing things up. "What *did* you do? This ain't you, boy. Not at all."

Curtis nods madly. "Right. It's not me. Least it didn't *used* to be, but it's sure enough me now, I'll tell you."

"So?" Phil says, gently removing the stump of the spliff from Curtis's hand. Then, with one finger he pushes him over.

Curtis tumbles, stays there.

"Tell me," Phil says.

There is a long wait.

"Get away from the door, Ma," Curtis yells, without stirring.

There is a brief clatter outside the door as she scampers away.

"So, tell me," Phil says, the last of the smoke rolling up over his top lip, over his face.

"No."

He stubs out the roach in his palm. "'Scuse?"

"You gotta go," Curtis says. He rolls from his side to his back, pauses, struggles to his feet. He wobbles. "I can't talk to you, Phil, you gotta go, now."

Curtis is gently tugging Phil by the hand, up off the bed. Phil doesn't resist, but when he is up, he gets up close in Curtis's face.

"What are you doing? You had me race over here . . . you smoked up all my dope."

Curtis is shaking his head. "I can't. I just can't. Tell you what, you call me. Right? Go home, get on the phone, call me. When you're not here, I can tell you."

"You crazy, Curt? That what you wanted to tell me, that you gone completely nuts?" Phil is being ushered out the door as he speaks.

"Just go and call me . . . or you wait there by the phone, and I'll call you. Right. There you go, Phil, I'll call you. Thanks again."

Phil is standing out in the hallway now, with Ma looking nervously over his shoulder. "No way," Phil says, "I'm calling you, the second I get home."

"Great," Curtis says, slamming the door shut and locking it. "Great, great, you call me. I'll be here."

He hits the floor, crawls on his belly like in a scene from Guadalcanal, until he reaches his bed, reaches under his bed, reaches his collection.

He pulls out one magazine. No, not that one, the other one. Yes. And that one, that one, that one.

They are spread out on the floor in front of him, and he is spread out on the floor in front of them.

He is investigating the scenes. His beloved scenes. The girl scenes, the girl-girl scenes. The guy-girl scenes. The guy scenes.

He is investigating himself, assessing himself, bits of himself pressed against the carpeted floor.

"Oh, my sweet Jesus," he says, flopping over, climbing to his feet, pulling on clothes.

He goes to the door. He barely touches the knob.

"Everything all right in there, son?" Ma calls.

He stalls, spins, makes for the window.

He wobbles in the window frame, lurches, reaches the telephone pole. He carefully makes his way down the spike ladder.

*   *   *

"What are you doing here? And what are you doing stoned so early in the morning? And you got any more?"

Curtis smiles warmly at Lisa, despite her flat tone. "Ah, you know me so well. Don't ya, Lis? I can always count on you, huh? To know me."

"No. My *mother* told me you were high when she came to get me. Said I shouldn't even let you in. I told her not to worry, because you were even more harmless this way."

"What? I am *not* harmless. This way or any other way."

Lisa closes the door behind them and walks to her bed. She is still in her shorty nightgown, and she does a little slide move as she hits the forest green satin bedspread.

"Of course you are," she says. "Totally harmless. But that's not a bad thing. That's why you were allowed in the house, for one thing."

He stands there, a little bleary-eyed, a little weavey. He points, about to make his stand.

But he is distracted by the fish.

He goes over to the very large fishbowl Lisa keeps as a sort of centerpiece to the room, resting like a great, bubbling head, an Apollo moon helmet on a plinth. He gets his face up close and stares in.

"Curtis," Lisa says sternly. "Curtis? If you knock over my fish . . ."

"I am not," he says.

"I *said,* if you knock over—"

"Harmless. I am in no way harmless. Don't I look like that scene from that crap movie you were watching? Where

DiCaprio is looking at what's her name through the fish tank? Don't you think I look like that?"

She sighs, an irritated sigh. "Not. You look more like one of the fish, actually. Especially the eye. And the lips. Sleep on your face last night or something?"

Curtis goes on anyway, staring close-up at the two fish in the bowl. One is a plump, bug-eyed goldfish with gentle, feathery, winglike fins that flutter lightly as it floats and swoops, comes to the surface for a noisy small bloop of air, then cruises down again, through the stone archway, brushing past the fake green sprig of foliage. He stares for a while at this, disappearing further and further into the water world of it, even making the same poppy-poppy mouth moves as the goldfish.

Then there is the other one, the blunt, myopic-looking creature, dashing past and catching Curtis's lazy eye. It is an altogether different creature, flattish, with stubbier fins and an all-over silver flesh that is so thin you can see the workings of its body inside. And the workings are not working so well. It seems to have a collapsed lung, or broken flotation device of some sort, because all he is able to do is lie for periods among the smooth green stones on the bottom, catching his strength, then suddenly bursting in a line to the top to gulp air or steal a fish flake, before sinking again, bouncing off the glass, coming to rest once more on the bottom.

Where it appears to lock Curtis in a penetrating, knowing stare.

"Hello," Lisa says from the other side of the glass.

He is momentarily stunned to see her, as if he had come to think he was alone with the fish.

But as his eyes focus in on the big-eyed, smiling Lisa, magnified by the glass and water, he becomes well reminded of why he is here.

"Nice nightie," he says.

She looks down at herself, giving him a view of the top of her head, magnifying the crooked part through her honey-colored hair.

"Thanks," she says. "You want to borrow it?"

"No," Curtis snaps, "that's not what I meant at all."

Lisa remains calm, if a little irritated with him. "Hello, Homer, I think I know that. I was offering you my nightie, but not for you to *wear* it."

The slowness of Curtis's uptake is exaggerated by the fact that they're having the conversation through the fishbowl.

"Oh," he says as both fish cross his view, going opposite ways. He goes momentarily cross-eyed. "Sorry, Lis. I'm just . . . a little weird and stupid right now."

"That's what makes ya great, Curt," Lisa says brightly, pulling her nightdress over her head and offering him a CinemaScope of her bare breasts.

Curtis, still crouched on the opposite side of the water, studies her for a while. The fish keep buzzing past, breaking his concentration.

"So?" Lisa says.

He straightens up, looking her in the face now. "Ya?"

"Ya," she says.

"Cool," he says.

"But," Lisa says as Curtis follows her smooth, naked bottom to the bed, "I'm going to put the movie on, *Romeo and J—*"

"No, *no,*" he barks.

"It was the smoke."

Curtis is not talking.

"Would you please stop worrying about it? Studies show, dope'll make you that way. Plays hell with your sexual function. If you hadn't smoked before you came over, you would have done fine."

He is sitting upright, has his arms folded across his chest, the covers pulled up tight to his belly. The movie is back on.

"What, are you mad at *me* now?" Lisa asks.

"No. Of course I'm not . . . could you turn *him* off, please?"

She snaps off the video, sits up in position right next to Curtis, leaning heavily, shoulder to shoulder with him.

"So what's the big deal?" she asks.

"The big deal? The big *deal,* Lisa? The big deal, is that I'm *gay.* All right? That deal big enough for you? Happy now? Well, you asked for it, and there you are. I'm gay. You happy?"

Lisa remains in position. If anything, she is leaning a little bit heavier into Curtis. There is a thunderous nothingness in the room at first, followed by a burst of noise out of the fish as they careen around the tank, knocking things over, possibly cracking the glass, making audible gasping noises as they breach the surface. An air force jet buzzes the house.

"Hmm," she says.

"Hmm?" he says. "*Hmmm,* Lisa?"

She clicks the film back on. "You're not gay, Curt."

"Stop that," he says, grabbing the remote and shutting it down again. "Don't contradict me. I'm telling you, I'm gay. Did you see me there? I didn't make it, and what's more, I didn't even come close. I *knew* I wasn't going to make it before I even started. I had as much chance of satisfying the *fish* as I did of satisfying you."

She slides back down into recline position. "You weren't gay last Sunday, if I recall," she says coolly.

"That's right, I wasn't. It happened last night."

One hand flies to cover her mouth, then two. When that's not enough to cover up the bursting humor all over her face, Lisa disappears under the covers.

Curtis sits stoically for a bit, watching the covers tremble, listening to murmurs of giggles.

"All right, all right," he says. "Cut it out. You're not helping me any."

She whips down the covers. "You don't need my help, you need a psychiatrist. You need a whole team of them, ya goon."

"I know," he says, "I was thinking that myself."

Lisa crawls from beneath the covers, crouches naked in front of Curtis, and gives him a loud slap on the forehead.

"Dodo," she says. "I meant you're crazy for thinking that you *went* gay just like that, overnight."

He points at her. "Exactly. Overnight. I had these dreams, Lisa . . . oh, awful stuff . . . all night . . . like I was in a gay porn film . . . like I was the *star* . . . doing stuff . . . stuff, I don't even know where I *learned* it, I swear. . . ."

She puts a hand on his chest to slow him down. "My god," she says, "feel you. You are going to have a heart attack."

"Good," he says. "I want a heart attack."

"Stop it. Listen, ya tight-ass—"

"Not anymore—"

"Shut up. Listen, Mr. Freakish Pent-up. Everybody dreams."

"Not like this."

"Ya, probably just like this."

"Well, I don't think so. But anyway, even if they did . . . the dreams would, like, y'know, *stop* when they woke up."

Slowly, like a naughty dog, Curtis allows his head to hang. He is staring down into his folded hands.

She raises his chin with two fingers. "And yours . . . aren't going away."

He shakes his head, Lisa's fingers sticking to him as if they are glued. He tries to look down again, but she forces him back up, forces his eyes to hers.

She speaks in an extra-sweet voice. "And you've been playing with yourself over it too, haven't you, honey?"

Curtis makes his move now. He squeezes his eyes shut.

She pulls him by the hair, and kisses him.

"It's all right, Curtis." She is grinning, near to laughing, when he opens his eyes. "It's perfectly all right."

"No, it's not," he insists. "I don't like that stuff. I don't think I should even be thinking about it. I don't think anybody should be thinking about it. It's wrong. I'm sorry, but it's wrong."

She scoots away from him a couple of inches, breaks all contact with him. "Now *that's* your damn problem, Curt. Not that you're gay, but that you're a jackass."

The phone next to the bed rings, and Lisa answers it, the sour look still hard on her face.

"Ya," she says, "so what do *you* want with him?"

In a few seconds she takes the phone from her ear and covers the mouthpiece. "You don't want to talk to your moron cousin right now, do you? That would be the *worst* thing you could—"

"Shit," he says. "Shit."

The small but mighty voice calls from the receiver, "Get on this goddamned phone."

Curtis takes the receiver while Lisa shakes her head and mouths, "Do not tell Phil."

"First," Phil barks halfway through Curtis's hello, "you send for me. Then, you smoke my dope. Then, you kick me out. Then, you lie to me and tell me you'll call me. Then, you scare your mother shitless by disappearing out the friggin' window. What the hell is wrong with you?"

"I'm gay."

"What? I mean, *what?"*

Curtis pulls the phone from his ear as Phil shouts. Lisa nods I-told-you-so and turns Leonardo DiCaprio back on. Curtis turns away, refusing to see.

"You heard me, Phil."

"Shut up, you're not gay."

"Shut up, I am. I'm telling you, I'm totally gay. I wasn't yesterday, but I goddamned well am now. I had dreams, Phil, like you wouldn't believe."

"Because you had dreams? Shit, boy, just get over it. We'll forget you ever said anything."

Curtis covers his eyes before the next bit, as if a powerful spotlight were being trained on him. "I haven't been able to stop the thoughts all day. It's happening still . . . right now, even . . . and Lisa won't stop putting on that damn movie. . . . And there's worse. Phil . . . now, listen, right . . . you were in my dreams, Phil."

Lisa instantly snaps off the set. Rolls over toward Curtis as if he were now the show.

"Me," Phil says in a slow, cold growl. "Me? Doing . . . doing what *you* were doing?"

"Doing it *with* me," Curtis says, a sort of death-rattle crackle interspersed with the words.

There is a long, deathly silence from both phone parties. Lisa has to muffle herself in the pillow.

"I—? I'm gonna kick your ass, boy," Phil says. "You hear me? I'm gonna give you the *cure.* I'm gonna give you such a beating—"

Chris Lynch

"Don't bother," Curtis says dejectedly, "I'll probably just like it."

He climbs over Lisa and hangs up the phone. She reaches instantly and unplugs it. Then she inches closer again to Curtis, and the two of them lie flattened, motionless but for very shallow breathing and heavy heartbeating. Her head is on his bare chest. His arm is around her.

"He's right," Curtis says.

"He's wrong," she says.

"It's wrong," he says. "I hate that shit."

"It's normal," she says.

They lie in silence. After too much of it she reaches for the remote. He grabs her hand to stop her.

He turns his head slightly, to be right in her ear. "You said everybody dreams it."

"Ya," she says.

"You? You, Lis?"

"Me? Of course, me. All the time."

The speed, and the volume, of his heartbeat is instantly trebled.

"Really?" he says, trying for a casual tone. "You? Thinking about, like, girls and girls?"

She turns her head to get a look at his newly brightened and alert eyes. She smiles into his smile.

"Ya," she says. "Think you can forgive me?"

He must force himself to pause, for respectable effect. "Well," he says, composure seeping out of him like sap. "Well, you know, Lis, you're probably right . . . like, that I should be a little more open-minded . . . and stuff . . . like."

He swings one leg over her, presses himself into her curved hip.

"Good of ya, Curt," she says, twisting slightly away from him. "Awfully good of ya."

He follows her closely, crossing into her territory, on the other side of the bed median.

He gets all whispery and close in her ear. "So then, y'know, when you are thinking . . . this *stuff* . . . what other girls are in there with you?" he asks. Suddenly busy, suddenly interested.

Suddenly cured.

Chris Lynch

about "The Cure for Curtis"

The idea for "The Cure for Curtis" came from twin strands I have been contemplating for some time now. The first—which, to be honest, I have been carrying with me for probably twenty-five years—is how rich and powerful one's fantasy life can be, all by itself. About how what we do in our subconscious life can feel so real and true when the sun comes up that we awaken with a new view of who we are. Whether we approve of that view or not.

The second strand, the one that ultimately brings on the conclusion of "Curtis," is about hypocrisy, and about the differences between male and female self-perception. It seems that males are generally so stuck to the idea of ironclad gender definition that we are willing to brand ourselves or others gay or straight on the basis of one act, one association, one thought, even. While at the same time, women appear less convinced of such certainties and are far more capable of uttering the liberating phrase "So what?"

So when these thoughts played out in this story, when the two strands met, what I wound up with was Curtis—a guy who can find the idea of a love scene between two women to be the ultimate turn-on, yet to whom the thought of himself in a similar scenario is cause for a nervous breakdown.

about Chris Lynch

Chris Lynch is the author of a number of acclaimed novels for young adults, including *Shadow Boxer, Iceman, Gypsy Davey,* and *Slot Machine,* all of which were selected as American Library Association Best Books for Young Adults and Quick Picks for Reluctant Young Adult Readers. His most recent novels are *Freewill; Gold Dust; Extreme Elvin,* a sequel to *Slot Machine;* and *Whitechurch.*

Originally from Boston, Chris Lynch now lives in Scotland.

That week in geometry we'd just started chapter 6, "Transformations." Mr. Randall had lectured about the difference between the preimage and the image. As I counted the slug-slow minutes in fifth-period English, staring at the blackboard but seeing Matt Matt Matt, I decided that before yesterday I had been a mere preimage, waiting to be transformed into my actual self. Mr. Randall told us each point in the preimage had to be mapped onto a specific point in the image; everything had to correspond. That meant I must still be the same arms and legs as yesterday, the same blood and muscles and cells. But it sure didn't feel that way.

The Acuteness of Desire

by Michael Lowenthal

At Richie Sander's tenth birthday party, Matt Thompson showed us all he was a faggot. He couldn't help it; those were the rules. Before we started strip poker, Jed Simmons had proclaimed, "Anyone who gets a boner is queer." He was a fifth grader, and so we believed him.

Bad luck buzzed around Matt like a swarm of no-see-ums. He lost his Bee Gees T-shirt in one round, a muddied tube sock two hands later. Three more bum deals in a row, along with Richie's royal flush, and Matt was done for, the first of the night to lose it all. With an odd calm he spread his cards on the carpet, then stood in front of us as Jed had instructed. His Fruit of the Looms were stainless but baggy. You couldn't really tell what they hid. Matt waited—three seconds, four, gathering breath—the way an actor pauses before a monologue. Then, with his thumbs tucked under the elastic, he tugged down the briefs.

No one giggled. No one pretended to look away. We stared at the bald truth of his erection, the way it seesawed like a forgotten fishing pole, some lucky fish stealing nibbles at hidden bait. Then Jed started chanting "Fa-ggot! Fa-ggot!" and we all joined, until Richie's mother called down to quit the racket.

"Time to hit the hay," Richie said, collecting cards and jamming them in the cardboard pack. Still wearing his pants, he inchwormed into his sleeping bag. The rest of us followed suit. Matt didn't say anything. He just unfurled his own quilted nylon bag and zipped his naked self inside.

It was six years before I had the nerve to call him.

Throughout junior high I was careful not to be seen near Matt. There were rumors about lots of kids, but we had seen the evidence about him with our own eyes. Anyone who chose to be friends with a known homo would have to be suspect too.

By tenth grade, though, the gang had split up. Richie's parents had sent him to military school in Virginia, and he only came home at holidays—each time with a little less personality. Hayes and Howard, the twins, were shipped to Chesterfield High when the county redrew the district lines. Jed lived in the new district too, but he got kicked out of Chesterfield three weeks into the school year. The word was, he was in a juvenile detention center in Fredericksburg.

That left me and Matt. He lived just four blocks up the street, both our homes solidly inside the Central High district. Still, it wasn't difficult avoiding him. Our parents weren't friends; his family weekended on the Eastern Shore. Matt took the bus to school, so I rode my bike. It wasn't bad except for band days three times a week, when I had to balance my bassoon case on the handlebars.

We didn't see each other much in school, either, because Matt got tracked into the advanced classes with the Chester Heights kids, and I was in the lower classes with the kids bused in from Cumberland. I didn't mind being in the dumb classes. The Cumberland kids were cool, not all uptight about straight A's and SATs. And the teachers pretty much didn't bother you as long as you physically showed up in class. School was a long blank between *The Flintstones* at seven and *Tom and Jerry* at three o'clock.

Except for geometry. That was the one bright spot in my day. I'd never been good at math, but geometry was different. I loved the precision, the absoluteness. The sum of angles in any triangle was 180, no matter how you drew it. Two parallel lines could never, ever touch. Even when they were off the page and out of sight, you knew you could depend on those lines.

I even liked the sounds of the words in geometry: *oblique, obtuse, acute, rhomboid.* I invented private meanings to correspond with my moods. "How are you feeling this morning?" I would ask myself, pedaling to school. "Acute," I would shout on a good day, "absolutely acute!" Or if I was a bit under the weather: "Man, I'm feeling kind of obtuse."

My favorites were the proofs. Instead of giving you a problem and making you flail around for an answer, the way they did in algebra, in geometry they told you the answer right off the bat. You knew exactly where you were supposed to end up; all you had to do was figure out how to get there.

One afternoon at the end of October, Mrs. Pruitt knocked on our classroom door. She taught AP calculus and was head of the math department. She almost never ventured to our end of the hall.

Mr. Randall, our teacher, walked to the door to huddle with her. They whispered awhile, and she showed him a piece of paper, maybe a report card or a test. Mrs. Pruitt's forehead looked like someone had clawed across it with a fork, the way my mother scraped lines into cucumber skins. When Mrs. Pruitt was angry or upset, the lines scrunched closer to her eyebrows. They were like that now.

Mr. Randall nodded and motioned in my direction. I looked down, pretending to study my notes. How could I be in trouble? I was acing this class; I'd gotten a 104 on our last test. Then it hit me: Mrs. Pruitt must be accusing me of cheating. She couldn't believe one of the dumb kids could score so high.

Her ratchet voice yanked my gaze back to the door. "This," she announced, "is Matt Thompson."

I jolted when she said the name. My fingernails dug arcs in my pencil.

"Starting today," she said, "he'll be joining your class."

Mrs. Pruitt crooked her bony arm around Matt's shoulders in a mechanical half hug. Then, as though afraid she would catch a disease if she stayed too long, she pushed him forward and strode from the room.

Michael Lowenthal

Mr. Randall patted Matt on the back. "Welcome to our class. You don't have any trouble with your eyesight, do you?"

"No," Matt said, staring at the floor.

"Fine. Then we won't do any rearranging. You can take the empty seat in the back, there, next to Jesse."

I flinched again. If Matt noticed me, he didn't show it. He cast a vague glance in my direction and started down the aisle. The desks were pushed too close together, so he had to hold his backpack above his head and shuffle sideways in a kind of retarded beginner's polka. His T-shirt untucked itself from his Levi's and bobbed over his belly button. A wispy but unmistakable line of hair swirled around the shallow hole, then crawled down to hide under the jeans. I had to turn away and face the wall.

After all the work I had put into avoiding him—morning after morning pedaling to school when I could have taken the bus; the long-cuts I devised, extra staircases I climbed, so I wouldn't run into him between classes—what had I done to deserve this?

As soon as I asked myself, I knew. It was an easy-as-pie if/then deduction, the simple stuff we learned back in chapter 2: Every consequence has an antecedent. And this, *this* was the consequence I'd been dreading all along, my inevitable punishment for buying a pack of Bicycles every week, inhaling the crisp new vinyl smell, and being able to picture exactly how Matt had looked when he lost the poker game . . . for keeping the eighth-grade yearbook under my bed and opening it to the page with his picture and studying it, then slamming the book closed with my dick over his smiling face, whipping it harder and harder until the pages stuck together . . . for thinking of him in the shower, on the way to school, during band . . . for wanting to do more than just think.

"Come on, Jesse. You of all people. Don't fail me now."

It was Mr. Randall. I had no clue how long I'd been zoning out. "Wouldn't dream of it, Mr. Randall," I said. "How can I possibly be of service?" That was good for a laugh from the class.

"Just the answer would be fine," he said.

"The answer to . . . ?"

"The sum, Jesse. The sum of the angles in a hexagon."

"Sure," I said. Everyone in the class was staring at me, including Matt. "It's, um, five hundred forty degrees?"

"Noooooo!" A classic Randall roar. "What the heck's gotten into you?"

Just then the bell rang. A tidal wave of kids swelled toward the door, but not before Mr. Randall could block the passage.

"Homework tonight is one through fifty at the end of chapter five. Odd *and* even, since even Jesse seems to need help with this material."

The collective groan was like a massive fart in my face.

The next couple of weeks, geometry was public humiliation. I was missing questions left and right, basic stuff like how to figure corresponding angles with parallel lines. When Mr. Randall asked me to draw figures on the board, I broke piece after piece of chalk, leaving unreadable, crumbly smudges.

Matt's desk was so close to mine that I could hear him breathing while Mr. Randall lectured. I could distinguish every blond hair on his forearm, how each one joined the pattern corkscrewing toward his wrist. The only way not to have Matt in my line of vision was to turn left and stare out the window. I took to doing this for long stretches, but Mr. Randall got wise and called on me every time I shifted.

Even at home, alone, I couldn't work. All it took was opening the textbook to that night's problem set and seeing a picture of, say, a trapezoid. I would remember the diamond pattern of the Adidas shirt Matt had worn that day in class, the way the fabric hung from his chest. A wiggly line in the text would make me think of his voice, how it wavered when Mr. Randall called on him. And then I'd be dizzy with other memories: his dick flopping from his underpants, the reddish vein barber-poling up its length, the tip that flared out like a Chinese pagoda's roof. In an instant my zipper would be down.

In all this time, Matt never said so much as "Excuse me" when he accidentally bumped my desk. I fluctuated between disappointment and relief. Did he think about me? Did I want him to?

The truth was, Matt was having such a hard time in geometry that he couldn't afford to think about anything else. Like Mr. Randall said, he couldn't tell a hypotenuse from a hole in the head. Watching Matt struggle with the simplest problems, I realized I didn't know him anymore. I knew the ten-year-old Matt perfectly, every naked feature seared into my retina's memory. But I had avoided him so long that this person across the aisle was a stranger.

I wanted to find out why he was failing math when he was a brain in every other class. I wanted to learn how his breath smelled first thing in the morning, when his teeth were still mossed with sleep. I wanted to know what he ate for breakfast, how dark he liked his toast. I wanted more.

It was a Thursday, one of those rainy fall afternoons when your socks get wet, and stay wet, and pretty soon your feet are flaking off in clammy chunks. I was counting the minutes until I could get home and climb into my sleeping bag in front of *Tom and Jerry*. At the end of geometry, when everyone mobbed the door, Mr. Randall yelled for me to stay.

I was prepared for the worst. We had taken a test the day before, and Matt had been wearing his pair of jeans that were falling apart at the knees. I had been so distracted by the hints of skin peeking through the cotton strings that when the bell rang I still had four problems left. I was certain I had failed.

"Thanks for sticking around, Jesse." Mr. Randall leaned on the very edge of his desk, impossibly balanced on a sliver of butt. He motioned for me to sit in the front row. His potbelly now loomed at eye level. "Listen," he said, "I don't know what's going on, but something's up. You've gone from my number one student to practically worst in the class."

"I'm sorry, Mr. Randall," I said. "I really am. You see . . ." But how could I possibly tell him why I was screwing up?

"Don't give me some dumb-ass excuse, all right? I don't care. I just want you back to normal."

"Me, too," I said. And I did. I wanted everything to be normal.

"Listen, you know Matt Thompson, the new kid? He's having a heck of a hard time. Just can't get a grip on the material. I suggested to his parents that they consider a private tutor. They asked if I knew anyone, and I recommended you."

The place just below my stomach seized. "But Mr. Randall," I said. "I mean, I'm hardly passing the class myself."

"Forget these last couple of weeks, Jesse. I've watched you enough to know you have an instinct for geometry. You're a natural. And you know, sometimes, if you have to teach someone else, your own mind kicks back in gear."

I was in high panic mode, desperate for any excuse to get out of this. Would Mr. Randall believe I had to look after my sick grandmother? Could I fabricate a job at Pizza Hut? But in the back of my mind I was already imagining Matt in my house, my own room, his lanky form lying on my bed. I thought of that first day he walked into geometry, shuffling past me with his backpack held high: the fuzzy whorl around his belly button, the waist of his Levi's kissing his hips.

"All set, then?" Mr. Randall said.

Someone had severed my nerve controls. I couldn't find my tongue. I simply nodded.

"Good. I'll tell Matt to expect your call."

"Hello, Matt? It's Jesse, from geometry." No—that made it sound like I was born in the Land of Geometry. "This is Jesse. We sit next to each other in math?" Too tentative. The rising inflection was how a girl would talk. "It's Jesse Feldman. Long time no speak."

I actually did that. I sat there by the phone, practicing what I would say when Matt picked up on the other end. "Measure twice, cut once," Mr. Randall always said before we started to sketch a figure on the board. I was measuring and remeasuring our possible conversation, wishing I had some kind of emotional protractor to tell me when I got it right.

When I mustered the courage to call, someone answered on the first ring.

"Hello?"

I would know that wobbly voice anywhere. It was the soundtrack of my dreams. But I had to play it cool.

"Hello," I said, "is Matt there?"

"Hey, Jesse."

"Matt?"

"Yeah. What's up?"

He had recognized me, too! Had he been noticing me after all?

"I guess I wasn't expecting you," I said. "I mean, for you to answer."

He laughed through his nose. "You dialed my number, didn't you?"

"It's just really good to hear your voice," I said, marveling at how easy this was. "It's been a long time."

"What's the deal with Randall?"

"Randall? I don't know, same old shit."

"That's why you called, right? The tutoring?"

"Oh. Sure, we can jump right into that if you want." I was trying to sound casual, trying to keep in mind how embarrassing this must be for an otherwise straight-A student. "When's a good time for you?" I asked.

"Listen, cut the crap, okay? Don't pretend I'm just dying to have you teach me retardo math."

Matt's words stung like tears. "Sorry," I said. "I just thought we might as well be friendly about it."

"The only day I can do is Wednesday," he said. "Every other day I've got soccer."

"Okay. How about four o'clock? My house?"

"Fine."

There was a long pause. I could hear Matt's impatient breathing. I was scared to say more, terrified that if I opened my mouth, I would confess everything.

"Is that it?" Matt sounded like a crabby checkout clerk at the Safeway.

The Acuteness of Desire

"Yeah. So I'll see you Wednesday at my house?"

Click. The line went dead. After all that measuring, I'd still managed to cut wrong.

He was wearing the same clothes he had been at school: a "Hands Across America" T-shirt, the jeans with holes in both knees, black Pumas. Those sneakers intimidated the hell out of me. They were for popular kids: guys who played in rock bands, soccer stars.

Matt swung his backpack off his shoulder and stepped inside. I asked if he wanted a snack, cinnamon toast or something, but he said he just wanted to study. I couldn't tell if he was still mad from the phone conversation or if he honestly wanted to buckle down.

We went to my room and sat on the floor. I couldn't believe Matt was actually here, in my room, on my rug. I had seen this picture in my imagination a billion times. I watched him checking out my posters: Bo Derek from *10* in her skimpy flesh-toned bathing suit; John Riggins diving over a heap of players into the end zone; the blacklight Led Zeppelin taped to the ceiling. They were posters kids had given me for birthdays and Hanukkah, stuff I was supposed to be interested in.

Matt unzipped his backpack with a raucous grating sound. "Any time," he said.

"Sorry," I said. "I was just trying to think of how to start."

We agreed to review the basics for a while, then concentrate on "Reflections," the chapter we'd just been tested on, and which Matt had flunked royally. At first I tried to be animated like Mr. Randall in class, turning the problems into little boxing matches that we had to get psyched up for. Matt just sat there, his face blank as an uncarved pumpkin. He got three-quarters of the questions wrong.

After half an hour of watching him fail, I tried a new approach. I answered a sample problem myself, showing Matt step by step how I solved it. Then I gave him a problem that was almost identical, only with different numbers, and told him to try. As he sat there, tapping pencil against chin, his textbook cradled in his lap, I couldn't help but stare. I was drawn to his knees, the skin visible through the tattered holes. They weren't tough and wrinkled like most people's, but smooth and strangely hairless. I wanted to bend over and tongue the patch of pink.

Something slammed into my thigh. I looked down: Matt's fist. Could he have guessed what I was thinking?

"I think I've got it," he said, handing me his notebook.

The page was a disaster of lines, like a first grader's attempt at modern art.

"Well, not quite," I said, rubbing my charley-horsed leg, trying not to let show how much his playful punch had hurt.

"Why not? There's, like, the mirror, and that makes these points reflect over here." Matt tried to navigate the inky jungle with his finger.

"Okay," I said, "I think I found the problem. See, reflection doesn't mean it has to be a mirror; that's just one kind.

The Acuteness of Desire

The images can be touching or overlap and still be reflections."

Matt's eyes dulled with confusion.

"Here," I instructed, "put out your right hand."

He did, and I put my left hand next to it, four inches away. I drew an imaginary line in the carpet halfway between them. "Now, you see how those are reflections, right?"

"Sure," Matt said, "just like a mirror."

"Right, but now watch. Move your hand so your thumb is right up against the line." As he moved his hand, I moved mine, too, until our thumbtips were millimeters apart.

"Still reflections, right?"

Matt nodded.

"Now, let's each move our hand over a couple more inches."

Matt hesitated. I thought he was going to balk, but slowly he slid his hand over and on top of mine, creating one giant, multifingered paw. With my free hand I redrew the imaginary line of symmetry—the same line as all along, but now spearing both our hands.

"They're still reflections," I explained, "even though they're overlapping. See?" I pointed to Matt's pinkie and then to mine. "These points are equidistant from the line of symmetry. So is this one"—I touched his ring finger—"and this one"—his index—"all of them."

I paused to let Matt contemplate the tangle of digits. It was only now, in the silence, that I realized what I had done.

Michael Lowenthal

After years of dreaming, my skin was on his skin.

"Wait, let me see if I have this right." Matt's voice was animated. He gripped my right wrist and pulled my entire arm closer. Then he put his left forearm up against it, touching from wrist to elbow. Magnetic sweat stuck us together.

"Now, obviously they're reflections like this," he said. "That's a mirror. But you're saying even if we do something like this"—he crossed his forearm over mine to form an X of flesh—"they're still a reflection?" He drew the line of symmetry with his bony index finger, then demonstrated how all of the corresponding points were equidistant. Goosebumps rashed the length of my arm.

"Yes," I said. "You got it. That's it."

"All right!"

We slapped a high five so hard it stung my palm.

This was my chance—while he was feeling good, while we were acting like friends again. *Ask him,* I pleaded with myself. *Ask him! Say the words you've rehearsed.*

Matt was sort of bouncing on the rug, twitching his legs. He stretched one so that his foot almost brushed my thigh. I was mesmerized by his sneaker's black sheen.

I must have sat there paralyzed a long time, because next thing I knew, Matt had grabbed his textbook. "Maybe I should quit while I'm ahead," he said, stuffing the book into his pack and zipping it. "It's getting kind of late."

I could feel my palms clamming. I wiped them discreetly on my socks. Matt was waiting for me to say something to indicate that he could leave without being rude. But I couldn't. I wanted him to stay this close forever.

Matt hoisted himself from the floor and brushed off his pants. "I guess I'll head home. Mom's probably got dinner ready."

He stepped toward the door, leaving me, and suddenly the words I had practiced in my head a hundred times were out loud, hovering in the air. "Um, Matt?" I sputtered. "Can I ask you something?"

"Sure, what?" He stood above me, his book bag draped casually over his left shoulder.

"Well, I know you're going to think this is goofy and stuff. But I wanted to ask if you think something is normal, or if it means I'm, like, totally weird or something."

Matt smirked. "You gonna tell me you fuck your dog?"

"No," I said. "No. Not like that." But I wondered if what I wanted to do wasn't just as bad. "In geometry? You know how our desks are just across the aisle? Well a while ago, I don't know, maybe a month? It was a day you were wearing shorts. You turned around to hand me a paper and—God, this sounds so dumb."

I could still stop. I hadn't lied yet, hadn't divulged the fantasy I'd perfected for just this occasion. But if I quit now, I knew I'd never have another chance. I stared at Matt's sneakers and kept talking.

"You . . . turned around and I could see your dick; it was hanging out of your underwear. I didn't even think about it. I mean, it's not like I haven't seen guys' dicks before, big deal. I didn't think about it at all until a couple of nights ago I was jacking off and suddenly it popped into my head. You know, the thought of your dick that day? I mean, I could picture it in my head. And I kept thinking about it, and . . ."

I looked up. Matt was still standing above me. His mouth hung open and his eyes were squinty, the way they got when he was stumped on a geometry problem. With a cold shudder I thought: *He could report me. He could tell Mr. Randall, everyone.*

"So, um, what do you think?" I said. "I mean, do you think I'm a total queer?"

For ten seconds Matt still didn't move. Then he dropped his bag. He sat back down across from me on the floor. "Nah," he said, stretching the syllable. "I think that's pretty normal. I don't think you should worry too much."

He had sat down three or four feet away from me, farther apart than when we'd been studying. I could tell he was trying not to seem freaked, but he didn't want to be too close to me either. I was about to say forget it, to pretend I'd never even brought it up, when he chuckled in a voice I hadn't heard before. It was almost like a little girl's laugh.

He said, "I've heard it's even normal for guys our age to jack off together and stuff. You know, just fooling around."

I looked at him, but he looked away. He stared at his own fingers rubbing his forearm, the same arm that minutes earlier had been pressed to mine.

"I guess I've never done that," I said.

"Me neither," Matt said.

The Acuteness of Desire   *145*

Then he glanced up directly into my eyes. I blinked, looked down, but when I raised my eyes again, he was still staring.

I don't remember which of us moved first. Maybe both at the same time. My hand met the smooth curve of his forearm, and his met mine. He brushed against me with the tips of his fingernails, up to the ticklish place on the inside of my elbow, then back down to my wrist. I moved my hand to his chest. I couldn't believe how hard the muscles were.

Matt let his body go limp so I could lift off his T-shirt. I tried not to catch his ears, and when his head came free, his hair was mussed from static. He looked like a little kid just woken from a nap. I flashed to Richie Sander's birthday party, to the image of Matt standing in his baggy underpants. And I understood now that what had hooked me was not just his boner, but the way he hadn't tried to hide it. He'd just stood there, accepting his fate.

Matt's chest was still tanned from the summer, a yellow brown that reminded me of fallen pine needles. I could smell his armpits, musty and sour like a trunk that hasn't been opened in years.

He slipped his hand under my shirt and whisked it up, a magician revealing the stuffed rabbit turned real. But he fumbled. The shirt got hung up on my nose, covering my eyes and head. I lost my balance and fell against him.

In seconds we had each other's pants off. I'm fuzzy on the logistics, if we each undid our own or if we let the other person wrestle with the buttons. But there we were, exposed, our jeans in a heap on the floor.

We just lay there a minute, getting used to the sheer fact of so much skin. I pressed close, wishing I could touch every inch of him at once. I could be his body-hugging wet suit; he could swim in me. I was so content with our simple proximity that I was startled when Matt reached down to my dick. I must have jumped, because he stopped and went rigid as a corpse. I sighed as obviously as I could to let him know it was okay. Then he started squeezing his fingers, making a circle, tighter and tighter, experimenting with different levels of pressure. *Cylinder,* I was thinking. *Base. Circumference.* I recalled the formula for calculating the volume of a solid object.

Matt had one leg locked between mine, so that his dick was smushed between his stomach and my thigh. As his hand jerked up and down on me, his hips humped with the same rhythm. He began murmuring under his breath, the way people talk in their sleep. "Oh my God. This is the best when it's flattened, and . . . shit . . . it feels like . . . it hurts but . . ."

Matt cried one last word, something like "now" or "no," and I felt a pool of warmth seeping on my thigh. *Acute,* I sang to myself. *Hyperboloid!* And then I came, letting Matt's hand catch it all.

"Wow," Matt said.
"Yeah. Wow," I echoed, not knowing what else to say.
"Phew," he sighed.
I made a similar sound.

The Acuteness of Desire

About three minutes had passed. I had no idea what we were supposed to do now; in my fantasies I'd never made it this far. It occurred to me that Matt might want to clean up, but I couldn't think of a way to suggest it without sounding gross. I was messy too, but in no hurry to wipe Matt's sticky gift from my leg.

Then Matt did this cool thing where he made his eyebrows do the wave, and we both started giggling. We laughed a long time, poking each other and trading goofy looks. It was like the end of a long plane ride, when your ears pop and you realize you've only been hearing half of everything all along. You want to yell at the top of your lungs, just to hear how loud you can be.

When we stopped laughing, Matt looked at me, and then at his own body. It was as if only now he recognized what we had done. He sat up and wiped his hand on the carpet.

"I better get dressed," he said. "It's almost dinnertime." He wriggled into his underpants and stood up.

"You can stay here for dinner," I offered. I was still naked, lying on the floor.

"No. My mom will want me back."

Matt already had his jeans on and was pulling up his socks. I dried myself with a T-shirt from my dirty clothes pile and rushed to catch up with him.

When we were both dressed, I walked Matt to the door and stopped him, holding on to his shoulders. I'm not even sure what I wanted to say, but it seemed important to have

Michael Lowenthal

the chance. Maybe I didn't want to say anything, just to hold him, just to kiss good-bye. As I leaned to his cheek, my mother's Oldsmobile turned into the drive. Matt pulled away.

"Hi, Mrs. Feldman," he called, waving, striding down the flagstone path. Then, over his shoulder: "See you, Jess. Thanks for the help on that geometry."

When my mother came in, I told her I had homework to finish. I went back to my room, locked the door, and lay down where Matt and I had been. I could still smell him, still feel his heat in the air. I picked up the T-shirt I had used to clean myself and draped it like a mask over my face. I sucked on the place where Matt's sperm had stained the fabric and let the exquisite bitter taste of him salt my spit.

School the next day was torture. I had Matt's schedule memorized, and I knew there was almost no chance we would see each other until geometry. We didn't even have the same lunch. Still, I spent each class squinting out into the hallway, hoping that if I stared hard enough, hard enough . . . I understood now what people meant when they talked about ghost pains in amputated limbs. Matt was a vital organ carved from my gut.

I didn't hear a word of Mr. Markowski's lecture on the Second Battle of Bull Run, or Señora Maldonado's explanation of the Spanish subjunctive. I was jittery, my whole body humming the way it feels when you drink a Coke too fast and all the carbonation bubbles up your nose.

That week in geometry we'd just started Chapter 6, "Transformations." Mr. Randall had lectured about the difference between the preimage and the image. As I counted the slug-slow minutes in fifth-period English, staring at the blackboard but seeing Matt Matt Matt, I decided that before yesterday I had been a mere preimage, waiting to be transformed into my actual self. Mr. Randall told us each point in the preimage had to be mapped onto a specific point in the image; everything had to correspond. That meant I must still be the same arms and legs as yesterday, the same blood and muscles and cells. But it sure didn't feel that way.

At last the bell rang. They should have nabbed me right then and there to do a commercial for the math department; I had never looked forward to geometry so much. I climbed the two flights of stairs to the top of C Building, gripping the banister to keep myself from running.

There were only three kids in the room so far, but thank God, one of them was Matt. Ruddy-cheeked Matt, hair jumbled and falling across the part, sublime dishevelment. I smiled reflexively at the sight of him, almost giving myself away. He sat at his desk, hunched over some papers. The way his head was tilted, all I could see of his face was the jawline, sharp and smooth as a knife.

"Matt," I said, and the release of that single word was like the vacuum seal popping on a can of tennis balls.

He pulled a pencil from behind his ear and scribbled some figures on the paper in front of him.

I made a fist and pretend-knocked on his head. "Hello?

Michael Lowenthal

Anybody home? Earth to Matt?"

He still didn't look at me.

"I almost called you this morning," I whispered. "Then I thought maybe it was too early. Would six thirty have been too early? I don't even know what time you get up."

Matt flipped to the answer section in his textbook, checked something, then erased a line on his homework. "I don't want to talk now," he said. "Not here."

I tried to breathe, but my lungs couldn't find air. A clutch of kids had strolled into the room, chattering about last night's *Murder, She Wrote.*

"Matt," I pleaded, trying to keep my voice down, but it cracked and came out a sob. "Matt. What's up? Come on."

"What?!"

The word hissed, bulletlike. Matt finally looked at me, but it was a look I didn't recognize. "Leave me alone," he said.

I don't even remember the rest of that class. I zombie-stared out the window or at my blank notebook page. I think Mr. Randall called on me somewhere around the end of the period, and I goofed the answer for the millionth time that month. Randall didn't even seem angry. He didn't expect much anymore.

Time was doing screwed-up things in my head, changing speed and warping my thoughts. I tried to review the previous afternoon, searching for anything to explain the way Matt was acting, but now the memories were fractured and staticky, like a storm-frazzled TV screen. Did I have anything to prove it had happened?

When the bell rang, I just sat there. Even when I heard Matt push back his chair and leave, I couldn't bear to look. As kids filed in for the next class I thumbed through my notebook, pretending I had something important to find. I studied my desk's graffiti—CINDY 'N' STEVE 2GETHR 4EVR, JD + GK = TLA—all the indelible evidence of other people's love.

"I'm not gonna sit on your lap."

I looked up stupidly at the girl standing above me, one hand fisted on her hip.

"*You* might be that hard up," she said, "but I'm not. That's my seat." It was Mandy Stevens, captain of the field hockey team. She'd never said a word to me before.

"Sorry," I said, "I was just . . ." But before I could think of an excuse, Mandy was already talking to the girl next to her about which lip gloss brand was best.

I shambled out into the hallway. By now it was empty except for the dawdling metalheads who skulked outside to smoke between classes and never hurried to get back. I was supposed to be in biology, my last class of the day, but I couldn't face another room of people. I slipped past Mrs. Pruitt, who was hassling some guy about the dirty pinups in his locker, and ducked into the stairwell.

I walked down one flight, two, another to the main floor, then past that to the very bottom, where the stairs ended in a door to the boiler room. I hadn't planned to go so far, but as I passed each possible exit I couldn't think of a good reason to walk out any one.

It was warm down by the boiler room, musty-smelling like a Laundromat. There was something soothing about the stale dank air. I slumped against the door, pulled my knees into my chest and fell asleep to the murmur of machines.

I woke just before his hand touched my shoulder. It was one of the janitors—Mr. Jackson, I think; we never bothered learning their names.

"Don't you have a class?" he said.

"No," I lied, then wondered what point there was lying to a janitor.

"Well, you can't sleep here anyway. Go on, get up."

"Okay, okay, I'm going." I shouldered my backpack and started up the stairs, my legs still leaden with sleep.

Below me the janitor opened the door to the boiler room. The furnace rattled furiously. I turned back, half expecting to see flames pouring out the door. Mr. Jackson stood holding the knob, looking up at me.

"Hey," he shouted over the noise. "You all right?"

"I'm okay," I said, resuming my trudge up the steps. "Thanks, I'm fine."

But I wasn't. I wasn't fine at all. I had just been curled at the bottom of a filthy staircase like some homeless bum sleeping on a steam grate. I looked bad enough for a janitor—a total stranger—to pity me. On top of that, I'd probably just lost credit for skipping biology and would have to repeat it next semester. All because Matt hadn't talked to me.

The bell rang just as I emerged into the ground-floor hallway; I'd slept through the entire period. The hall flooded with people, and I skirted along its edge. I tripped over something—a backpack, maybe, or a leg—and had to grab on to some random girl to keep from falling. I didn't say anything, just kept moving until I was out the front door and down the concrete steps. I ran past the bike racks, staying close to the buildings. He'd be headed toward the gym for soccer.

As I neared A Building, I saw him. He was on the steps, alone, descending quickly. I don't think he saw me. I don't think he could have. But at the bottom of the steps he turned right, away from me, taking the long way around.

I followed him, trying to gain ground, but he was almost jogging. He cruised past the tennis courts and the picnic tables, turned another right at the baseball diamond. His blue windbreaker fluttered like a kite's tail behind him. It seemed he might lift into the sky and soar away.

When I caught up to him, we were in back of the school, near the football fields.

"Matt," I yelled, straining for breath.

I was only five feet away, but he acted as though he hadn't heard.

"Matt," I said again. "Quit running away from me."

He turned, just enough so I could see the cold flash of his eyes. "I'm not," he said. He increased his stride.

"You're not? Then what do you call this?"

Now we were in the parking lot between the gym and the football fields. Cars in various states of disrepair were strewn around the gravel-dusted pavement, junkers that people had donated to the auto mechanics class. Matt still hadn't slowed. I pulled him by the shoulder, hard, and made him stop.

Matt yanked my hand away and squared off in front of me. "Fuck off!" he yelled.

"*You* fuck off," I yelled back. I wasn't giving any ground. I stared until Matt turned his eyes down. He scraped loose gravel under his sneaker, rousing a small gray cloud. We could hear the JV cheerleaders, two fields away, practicing for Friday's homecoming.

"Why are you being like this?" I said.

Matt spat and rubbed in the spittle with his shoe, drawing an angle that I instinctively measured at 30 degrees. "I'm not being like anything," he said. "And I'm not running away from you. Do you think I even care about you that much?"

"Matt, I can't believe you're doing this." I was still trying to sound tough but my voice choked. I was close to crying. "You're acting like yesterday didn't even happen. But you liked it. I know you did."

Matt laughed in my face. "Bullshit, Jesse. You're dreaming. Yesterday was sick, and so are you."

Now I was crying, the tears turning Matt into a blurry blue mess. "But what about fourth grade?" I said. "Richie's party. Don't you remember?"

"I don't know what the fuck you're talking about." Matt turned and ran back the way we had come.

There was a menacing rumble inside the gym. The locker-room doors burst open and a horde of football players stampeded out. They rushed toward me across the parking lot, their cleats clacking a hailstorm on the pavement. They were huge in their blue-and-gold uniforms, helmets tipped back like molting insect shells. They streamed past, knocking me with their padded shoulders. I had to jump away to keep from being crushed.

When finally they had passed, I stood alone with the abandoned Pintos and piles of hubcaps. I was looking for the place in the gravel where Matt's shoe had scuffed the angled groove. It seemed important to find that trace of him, that mark I had seen him make. I searched all around me, but the football players had trampled everything. The wind shifted, swirling from the practice fields in toward the building. I could hear them grunting through their first round of calisthenics.

about "The Acuteness of Desire"

Love is so brutally uncertain. I've always wished there were guidelines to follow—some mathematical formula, plottable on an *xy* graph; a set of questions for which there were "correct" answers at the back of each chapter. For gay people things are especially confounding, because society doesn't even hand us the right textbook!

In "The Acuteness of Desire" I wanted to write about a gay boy who, after careful calculation and measuring, finally musters the courage for romance—and how painful it is when he learns that desire is, in fact, immeasurable, because you can never know the other side of the equation. If anything, I guess desire is asymptotic (one of my favorite geometrical terms): like the curve of a hyperbola approaching its limit, we can get closer and closer to figuring it out, but no matter how long we try, we'll never quite get there.

about Michael Lowenthal

Michael Lowenthal graduated from Dartmouth College in 1990 as class valedictorian. Three years later—after stints of dishwashing, bartending, and working at University Press of New England—he began his career as a full-time writer and freelance editor. His first novel, *The Same Embrace,* was published in 1998. His short stories and essays have appeared in the *Kenyon Review,* the *New York Times Magazine,* and the *Crescent Review,* and have been anthologized in more than a dozen books, including *Best American Gay Fiction.*

Michael Lowenthal currently lives in Boston and teaches writing at Boston College.

Ark was a funny name for a band. I wanted Michael to name his group Trolls because of a dream I had a long time ago, but I felt too weird to tell him about the dream and the troll bumps.

The sixth time we had sex—yes, I was counting, because it was important for me to tally my emotions, and because I'd never had sex with anyone before—I almost told him.

Troll Bumps

by Shelley Stoehr

"*Please*, Betty," I whispered to the stolen car, my sister's Nova, when it stalled at the Main Street stoplight. Betty was the name I'd given the car while taking it from Maggie's driveway, as I pushed it slowly over the gravel so the engine wouldn't disturb the 3 a.m. silence. I named it Betty so I could talk to it and maybe not feel so lonely on the long trip ahead. It wasn't *really* stealing, because I left my sister a note. I was *borrowing* Betty to get to Michael, and his band, his pigtails, his spidery hands, and the magical little troll bumps on his back.

Once Betty was warmed up, she drove smoothly. By noon I was in Ohio, chewing a hot bagel while I waited for a Sam Goody in Cleveland to open. Betty had a tape player I'd never tried.

Because Cleveland had been on Ark's tour, I was pretty sure I'd find their tape here. I would've seen them play if I hadn't been so slow in deciding to follow them. But it wasn't until Michael had been gone almost a week that I knew for sure I couldn't exist without him. Maybe if he'd answered the messages I left for him on his voice mail, or maybe if, when

I found what hotel he was staying in, he'd picked up the phone sometime during the thirty-five rings, maybe then I could've stayed home and waited for him to come back. But no contact was impossible. It only reinforced a deep fear that he wasn't ever coming back. It was up to *me* to make six months of sex and warm cuddling more than just six months of sex and cuddling. It was up to *me* to become his girlfriend. I wrote pages of letters every day, and when my notebook was finally full of unmailed love, I emptied my savings account, packed my coolest, sexiest outfits, and borrowed Betty.

As I waited at the register for my change, with *Two by Two,* Ark's first album, in my hand, I thought of Michael's soft, lazy voice singing from one of his songs, "I feel your breath behind my ear, / And where you are, I go too. / I won't be swallowed by me and fear / Or the sharp-toothed beasts made by you."

I go too, Michael.

Ark was a funny name for a band. I wanted Michael to name his group Trolls because of a dream I had a long time ago, but I felt too weird to tell him about the dream and the troll bumps.

The sixth time we had sex—yes, I was counting, because it was important for me to tally my emotions, and because I'd never had sex with anyone before—I almost told him.

Michael sighed very quietly, almost whistling, which was how I knew he came. He was never noisy in bed, and I

Shelly Stoehr

couldn't just *feel* what was happening to him. I had to note little clues like his cum-sigh so I could respond but still keep most of my attention focused on memorizing Michael as he was and also recreating him as my soul mate.

Michael's forehead sank down and rested against mine while I examined the knobby slope of his pelvis with my hands. The size of his butt cheeks as compared to my cupped palms was duly noted in my mind, and I ran my thumbs across his lower back. Satisfied that his actual skin, bumpy and coarse and alive, fit my mental picture, I said I loved him.

"What?" he said.

I thought he heard me the first time, so I didn't answer right away, I just kept tracing the bumps on his back.

"What did you say?" he asked, brushing his fingertips over my eyebrows, but not as studiously as I touched him.

I was amazed that he could touch me so casually. Where did he get the balls? I mean, how could he be so unafraid of how he'd feel if he never got to have sex with me again? How could he not need to memorize me in case of future catastrophe?

"Michael, I love you," I said, smiling so he wouldn't think I was chickenshit, scared to death of him not saying it back, which I knew he wouldn't.

He didn't.

But he smiled and kissed my knuckles, up my arm, around my elbow, under my shaggy hair where the butterfly barrette had fallen out, and finally on the tip of my nose.

Troll Bumps

Then he asked, "Why?"

I said, "Because you have the troll bumps," extra quiet.

"What?" he asked, this time because he really didn't hear me.

Instead of telling him about my dream, I said, "What do you mean, why do I love you? I just do. You make me happy."

"I was just wondering," he said then, and we went back to kissing. And I went back to studying, evaluating, storing, and planning Michael for now, then, and maybe later.

I dreamed about the troll bumps a year ago, before I met Michael. It was before Ark was even a band. In fact, Michael was still living with his father in Florida when I first dreamed about his troll bumps.

In my dream I heard my own name, "Grace . . . Grace," weaving down through the high branches in a twisted forest and coming up from the leaves I was walking on. My name sounded like it belonged to more than just me, swirling around with a long *Ssss* at the end. As I searched for the voice I had a strong feeling that it was somehow wrong and that I shouldn't find the person calling me, but I followed the sound anyway because I also felt something amazing on the verge of happening.

The first few times I had this dream, I woke up smiling with anticipation, but no closer to finding the voice. Deep in the back of my mind was a sadness that I can understand now, when I'm awake, too clearly. Sometimes I wonder what would have happened if I'd stayed in the forest and not wandered into the dream cave the next time I heard the voice in my sleep.

It wasn't exactly a cave, it was more of a big, rusty pipe with water dripping in thick, mossy drops from the sides. "Grace, Gracccccce" came from deeper inside, and now the voice sounded like it had been filtered through molasses. Like Michael singing.

Again I woke up before reaching the voice, and when I tried to go back to sleep, I could dream only about waiting on line for Tori Amos tickets, and trying to catch a plane to Iowa but missing it, and eating a fish taco, whatever all that meant. So I started going to bed earlier, hoping for the dream to come again. When it did, even my dream self was desperate. I ran through the cave-pipe, and the voice stopped. It was dark in my dream then, and I couldn't see anything, but I could smell the most woozy-sweet scent. Suddenly I was being caressed by someone I couldn't see, but when I rubbed his back, there were little bumps above the ridge of his pelvis and next to his spine. When I woke up, I called them troll bumps because they were magical, somehow, like fairy wings but more musky—like bumps on trolls. In the dream I was so intensely in love and so utterly devastated at the same time, and the bumps were like braille, telling me why, only I couldn't read them yet.

I still couldn't, but I wanted more than anything some more time to learn. Which was why I had to follow Michael, and Ark, until I caught up and figured it all out.

*   *   *

Troll Bumps

Betty's tape player had autoreverse, so I let Ark's tape keep playing until my breath naturally flowed in with the eerie tones of Michael's guitar and out with the heavy *bwung* of the bass. After a while it was hard to feel what was my own heartbeat and what was drumming on the tape. Even Betty sped up and slowed down accordingly. I wished there were something I'd created that could do the same thing to Michael. If I could paint, I might have given him a picture, which he could be mentally disappearing inside of now, thinking of me. If I could dance, he might see a curve in the road and remember the arch of my leg, lifted high. But I'm not very artistic, so there wasn't anything he could've taken with him that would haunt him and make me impossible to forget. I could only hope that maybe he'd saved the notes and letters I used to write him, and between gigs on the road would unfold and fold and unfold and read them until the paper was thin and tearing at its creases.

About twenty minutes short of Toledo, Ohio, it started to rain. Then it turned to hail, ice being driven into the windshield like tiny cannonballs. Betty coughed and spit, and I had to get off the interstate. Pulling into a Motel 6 parking lot, I waited inside Betty until the storm passed. It tapered off to heavy rain, then light rain, and finally drizzle. When the sun came out, like a new world, Betty was left with a thin blanket of sky droppings all over her windshield. The wipers only smeared it into gray haze, but I could see well enough to drive, and I didn't want to stop yet. I wanted to catch up to Michael soon, and I knew he'd be performing in

South Bend, Indiana, tonight. If I skipped dinner, I could be there about when the show was finishing. I'd lean against Ark's tour van in a vinyl miniskirt with a black net top and maybe no bra. I'd tap the heel of the same go-go boots I'd worn the last night Michael was in New York.

But Betty wouldn't budge.

"Come on, girl, don't you want to see Michael?" I begged.

The wetness rose off her hood in steam from the afternoon sunlight, and she seemed to purr under me a little, but she wouldn't start. Even when I started crying, the key made only a useless little scraping sound when I turned it. I remembered my sister used to sometimes miss work when it rained, because Betty was picky about the weather. I could've called a mechanic, but I knew Betty still wouldn't go until she was ready, so instead I checked into the motel.

Although it was now almost hot outside, inside my room it was cold and damp like a cave. The thin blanket and rough bedspread didn't keep goose bumps from rising on my scrawny legs and bony arms. I picked at scabs under the covers and tried to watch the TV that jutted out of the wall. But the storm must've fucked with the reception, and all I got was a scratchy *Alice Doesn't Live Here Anymore,* which scared the crap out of me. I felt sick to my stomach, wondering what would happen if Betty didn't start in the morning and I got stuck here, screaming distance from the interstate, in Ohio, for God's sake. I got another chill and more goose bumps thinking about it. Turning the TV to a station of static, I imagined aliens landing and was almost comforted.

Curling up on my side, I put my thumb in my mouth and sucked hard. I was trying to fill myself with myself. By pulling the blanket over my head and drawing my body parts as close to my center as I could, it almost worked, and touching my cold toes was almost like holding Michael's always freezing feet.

We were lying in bed, and Michael looked sweetly goofy with the pigtails on one side of his head squished into the pillow, and on the other side, one elastic barely hanging on to bleached, split ends of hair. The elastic had completely fallen off his fourth pigtail, but his hair still poked out from his scalp in a ragged curl. His eyes were open, but he wasn't looking at me.

"What are you thinking?" I asked, although I was afraid to know.

"Nothing," he said. "Lots of things."

"Like what?" I asked, smiling and trying to move into his vision.

He continued to look through me. "I don't know. I have a lot on my mind," he said.

Stretching my legs down, I curled my toes over his feet. A shiver scurried up my spine.

"Your feet are so cold," I said. I kissed his hair, and his eyes refocused on me.

He brushed his fingernails, longer than mine and painted

with black polish, against my chin. "All the blood must've gone to my heart," he said.

I thought that was his way of saying he loved me, and I licked his eyelash. Crawling to the bottom of the bed, I rubbed my hands on his feet, trying to make them warm. After a minute I couldn't breathe anymore, deep under the sheets like that, so I squirmed back up. When I ran my thumb over Michael's thin, pink lips, he nuzzled my hand and ended up sucking my thumb like a perfect child.

That was what I thought about as I sucked my own thumb, alone in the Motel 6. The thumb Michael had kissed. The thumb that had once stroked the troll bumps on his back. It suddenly occurred to me that when Michael said all the blood must've gone to his heart, he'd meant it literally. It wasn't where love came from, it was just an organ that pumped blood.

The next day Betty was running again, and I should've been feeling good about that, but instead I felt itchy and awkward. I wanted to shed my skin. Something felt wrong with the universe, or at least with me in it. I think it was because the memories I'd kept hidden, of Michael as less than perfect, kept trying to creep into my mind.

After spoiling Betty at a gas station, filling her with gas and oil and cleaning her windows, I tried to pull Ark's tape out of the deck. The radio would be good for a change. Michael didn't have to be my reason for everything—I could enjoy this trip into the heart of the country for itself and the smoothness of the road, the breeze slipping through my bangs and tickling my ears.

But the tape wouldn't come out. I drove for eight hours listening to Michael's molasses-soaked voice slide effortlessly across notes. "If I promise to miss you," he sang, "will you leave me alone?"

"I'll think about it," I said to the tape.

Meanwhile, my voice cracked trying to hit a high note, singing along to, "Plastic cup, scratched and stained, / Never empty, never full. / Am I cream and sugar? Or am I just a pain?" Coming from my mouth, it sounded so stupid. I guess I couldn't project very well. *Unless,* Betty whirred into my head, *it's not you—could be the whole song just sucks.* I had to smile at that.

When I stopped for the night, I was in Indiana, a day late. Although I was hot and frazzled, and incredibly bored with *Two by Two,* which would probably run through my head for the rest of my life, I still felt somehow in tune with the world and calm deep in my chest. In my room I took a long time peeing, not rushing like I usually do.

For the next two days I made a point of stopping often to look at the world, trying to find a connection with it again. Ark's tape was still stuck in Betty's tape player, and Michael's voice oozed through me, sloshing around in my head like old bathwater that still smelled slightly of lilac bath salts. But the more I drove, the less I could conjure him in my mind.

As he slipped away from me I felt like I was losing a part

Shelly Stoehr

of myself. I could still feel the impressions his troll bumps had left in my fingertips, but not the magic. Was it true—out of sight, out of mind?

Maybe I was only tired. But I couldn't help worrying whether I'd still love Michael by the time I caught up to him. My judgment was starting to feel out of whack.

When it got to be too much, and my hands started to shake on the steering wheel, and I felt ready to cry—which I couldn't do, since I might not be able to stop—I pulled off I-80 into a piece of a town to get back in sync with the world and maybe get some of my dreams back, the ones that were for Michael.

There were fat people everywhere, which was a relief. Their fullness was comforting to my emptiness. I parked Betty and went into a place called Porky's. At the counter I stared into the mirror at whole families of pink, smiling, flabby faces. When the kitchen door swung open to let a big-busted, round-hipped, permed-hair waitress through, I caught a glimpse of the jowly cook spreading barbecue sauce with sausage fingers. Everyone in the place seemed to be whistling or humming or talking loudly about something, fingers and lips dripping. No one paid attention to my shaggy, bleach-burned bangs or to the curve of nine earrings that ran up each of my ears. Being cool didn't matter, like it had with Michael, but it wasn't a bad thing either, like it had been at home, with my sister, Maggie. All these smiling people made me wonder if they knew a special secret of life. Maybe the soul dwells in flab. That's why Michael couldn't care; he was too skinny. And maybe that was why I was getting more and more numb all the time. I wasn't pigging out enough.

So I finished a whole plate of ribs, then forced a hot piece of gooey pie down too before leaving. My fingers left sticky prints on Betty's hood when I climbed up to soak in the sunshine. There was green everywhere, and I wanted to roll in the shiny grass in front of an oddly cheery funeral home, even though I knew I should be heading back to the interstate, chasing Michael. Maybe I just had to *get there,* and then all the love would come back, for both of us. I could again be tingling, instead of shivering, when I thought of him.

While I sat there, trying to digest lunch, a guy approached and climbed up on Betty's hood to sit next to me. He didn't ask permission, just ran his fingers through slicked-back hair and flashed me a smirk. The cigarette pack he had rolled in the sleeve of his T-shirt pressed against my arm, and I felt like he was sitting too close, but I didn't bother to move away. His cockiness was annoying, and I should've told him to get the fuck off my car, and what was it with that James Dean-wanna-be look anyway?

But I felt like I was fading. I wasn't wanting Michael like before, and not wanting anything was scaring the fuck out of me. Maybe this guy was what I needed. Maybe it would bring me back to my senses, having someone stare at me with goofy eyes. It was a look that wasn't particularly affectionate, but which at least showed interest.

Smiling, I said, "I'm Grace."

"Daniel," he said, revealing perfect white teeth.

A plus, I told myself.

"Where are you from, Grace?"

"New York," I said. I looked at him closely and noticed he wasn't bad looking, except for the pretentiously retro hairstyle. I tried to open my mind and feel some lust and wanting, but I only felt sad. His company was making me lonelier than before.

Leaning into me, just slightly, not too intimidating, Daniel asked, "Going somewhere? I mean, most people are just passing through here."

"California, maybe," I said.

"Nice place," he said.

"Have you been there?" I asked, trying to be friendly and hoping that a regular conversation with a real person would snap me away from the past-and-future Michael I'd been living for.

"No," Daniel said. "But I've heard stuff."

I nodded.

We sat for a while, watching cars pass by. I tried to think of something to say, like maybe asking him what he did for a living, except that I didn't really care. So I started to imagine having sex with him, just figuring out in my mind if it was possible for me to do that. Trying to decide if it would be worth it. Would I like it? Would it make me feel better? Could I fall instantly in love with Daniel, like I did the first time I kissed Michael? Would it be the same with any guy—

was fairy-tale love just a hoax anyway? Daniel couldn't possibly have the troll bumps, but I wondered what other interesting abnormality I might find on his body. If I really looked, there might be something magical there.

"You wanna take a walk?" I asked.

"Yeah, sure," he said, and we started down the road.

I let my feet push the dirt at the side of the road into tiny dust plumes. We came to a strip mall with a Long John Silver's in front. I stopped under the sign, feeling not like a decent-looking girl who might get laid by a decent-looking guy in a small town, but more like an otherworldly creature. A creature speckled with bright yellows from the sign.

"Want to get some food?" Daniel asked. "I feel like french fries."

Although I was still full from lunch, I could feel myself nod, and I followed Daniel into the restaurant, still not really part of the real world. Inside myself, I was watching, seeing what would happen next.

Daniel got fries, and baskets of fish and shrimp. Not until we started eating did I jolt back to my whole self. It happened when Daniel was opening a foil packet of ketchup over his fries. The watching part of me saw his hands; the thinking part of me remembered and laid an image of Michael's hands over Daniel's, like a film transparency, and I suddenly switched into total awareness. Because Daniel's hands were wrong. They were small and pale, almost hairless, with dainty little oval fingernails. I didn't want to hold those hands, I wouldn't want to run my lips over them, and I couldn't imagine them touching me. Poking me, maybe.

Michael's hands were older than the rest of him, craggy from working in his mother's garden. He loved plants. His fingers grew out of spade-shaped palms, long and slender but strong, like vines. They widened at the tips, and his fingernails, always painted black, were big, ridged, and sturdy.

I shut my eyes and rubbed my own hands together, feeling Michael's presence so strongly I could smell his hair. As the memories flooded back I felt woozy. I wasn't sure anymore if I wanted them back.

"Are you okay?" Daniel asked.

I could *feel* the creases in Michael's knuckles, as though I were holding his hand between mine, stroking it. My heart clenched into a knot in my chest while my stomach fluttered below. But the weird thing was, I wasn't feeling Michael like I did before. The memories were like a person's life flashing before her eyes in perfect clarity, right before she dies.

"I'm not feeling so well," I said. "I think I better get out of here."

"I'll walk you back to Porky's," Daniel said.

I didn't want to be rude, so I let him wrap my shrimp and carry it for me. Back at the rib place, standing next to Betty, Daniel gently brushed his hand against my arm. I felt terrible, but what could I do? It just wouldn't work, even as an afternoon fling. I wished I could explain, but I couldn't tell a stranger, "You seem nice, and you're decent looking, but I'm sorry, your hands are wrong."

Troll Bumps

So I smiled and tapped my watch, like I was in a hurry. It was a lame excuse, but Daniel didn't seem too surprised. He didn't even try to scam his way into the car. Handing me my shrimp, he smiled too and turned to go.

"Nice meeting you," he said. "Hope you feel better soon. Hope you like California."

When he was gone, and I was alone in Betty, I peeled the batter off my fried shrimp and ate it, leaving the pink shellfish in the paper basket, cold and greasy and smelly. But even the fishy smell and sudden desire to puke couldn't make me stop breathing in Michael in my head. I couldn't see him anymore, though, or hear his voice. It was like being back in the dream cave.

I started Betty, actually relieved to hear *Two by Two* again, because it was concrete and forced Michael's voice back at me. Still, the music couldn't fill me with desire again. Instead, it sucked my soul in deep and rock hard, a frozen pea stuck in the center of my diaphragm making my breath catch. I pointed Betty back toward the interstate, goose-bumped, pale, worried, and shriveled around a full belly of greasy food.

The entrance ramp was in sight up ahead when suddenly Betty got quiet. No more Ark. No more coughing engine. No more wind rushing past. Only the sound of her tires slowing over pebbles at the side of the road as I drifted to a stop. I put her into park and tried to start her again. Nothing. I pressed the gas pedal three times fast, and then once slow, turned the key again, and still nothing happened.

Shelly Stoehr

"Come on, Betty," I said. "Look, the sun is out! It's a beautiful day for driving! What's wrong?"

After a while I got up and looked under the hood, but I didn't know what I was looking for. Hoping Betty had only wanted some attention, I tried to start her again, but she wouldn't go. While I was twisting the key over and over, frantically, and probably totally flooding the engine with gas, a woman in a white Range Rover pulled up behind me and came to stand by my window. Smiling generously, she offered to help. When the battery wouldn't jump-start, she tied Betty to the back of her car with some rope. I didn't say a word, because she seemed to know what she was doing. Since I was totally clueless about *everything* at this point, I was glad to have someone around who had a plan.

"There's the most wonderful mechanic only a half mile from here," she said.

While I was crinkling my forehead, mentally counting and budgeting the three hundred and change I had left, all the money I had to get me to Michael, she slowly and carefully dragged Betty and me to Gabriel's Auto Service.

"Gabe! You here?" she called into a cool, deep hole of a workshop.

"Out in a few," called a voice from behind us, perky with a light upbeat. I looked and saw feet sticking out from under an orange VW Bug, Converse low-tops with holes in the soles and greasy bits of sock poking out. The feet wiggled hello, or maybe they just itched.

"Are you going to be okay?" the woman asked me.

Troll Bumps

"Sure," I said, shrugging. It wouldn't help to start crying now. I wasn't even sure I could cry.

As the woman untied Betty the voice under the Bug said "You can wait in the shop if you want."

The voice had a way of making me feel better. It almost sounded like there were little bells tinkling in the background. The Converse sneakers pointed toward the cavelike workshop, and I went inside the dark, cool moistness that smelled like grass clippings and greasy metal.

It seemed like I waited for a long time, sitting on a backless stool with my hands flattened between my knees. Although I had hated metal shop in school, and the way everything was gray and slick, it didn't bother me here. I liked the unfinished pressed wood that just leaned against one wall, not even nailed on, with lumber-shop markings still scrawled over it. Written on the wood there were phone numbers—RAONDTABLE (crossed out and corrected to ROUND-TABLE) PIZZA, PETER (written heavily, like it had been traced over many times), GOODYEAR TIRES, and other numbers that weren't labeled. Next to the phone, which was smudged with black fingerprints, was a shabby birthday card, and tacked under that was a signed photograph of Christopher Lloyd as Jim from *Taxi.* There was a Harley calendar, still opened to June. Amidst the clutter on the workbench was an open pizza box with one slice still in it, amazingly bug-free, since I could see insects swirling all over the place in the sunlight outside.

Swiveling the stool around, I stared for a long time at the

humongous machinery—the drill press, scattered with shiny shavings of metal, was all I recognized. A tilting shelf against the wall was stacked with containers of oil and lubricants, and other things so dirty I couldn't read the labels. Still, there was an order to it all. And a sense of complete *belonging.* All this mess *belonged* to someone, had been accumulated and arranged just so, and had some purpose or meaning. It felt very peaceful.

A scraping outside signaled me that Gabriel was coming out from under the VW. He looked at Betty once and then came to the doorway of the shop. As he brushed dirt off the back of his blue coveralls his blond hair swung in strings like a Muppet's. He was thickly, *proudly* built, with a round face.

But what stood out most were his hands. As he came closer I could see the many heavy lines accented with grime. The fingers were spatula shaped, and the knuckles were gnarled and prominent. His hands were *right.*

His hands are so right, I thought again.

"So," he said, grabbing a rag from the workbench. He picked it up without looking, knowing where it would be. Just as I'd thought—the shop might look like a mess, but everything had been placed just so, and after wiping his hands, Gabriel flung the rag back exactly where it had been.

"What am I supposed to do for you?" he asked.

Shrugging, I went back to staring at his hands. My heart was beating hard, almost shaking my ribs.

"I hope you're not in a hurry to get somewhere in *that*," he said, pointing to the Nova with a perfect index finger.

"Not really," I said.

"Were you headed somewhere?" he asked. With the sun framing his head in a golden glow, he looked like an angel in coveralls.

I shrugged. "California, maybe. Not really. I don't know. Somewhere, I guess." I could hardly speak as my insides filled with something, a *wanting.* I felt like I was swelling into a new person.

Gabriel shuffled closer, wiping sweaty grime from his forehead with his sleeve. "Is someone waiting for you there?" he asked.

"I'm pretty sure he's not waiting," I said. My feet curled around the base of the stool, trying to keep me from spinning off into heaven. Gabriel smelled earthy, like wet leaves at the bottom of a pile. I wanted to bury myself in him.

Just like that, Michael's feathery smell seemed too insubstantial for me. *Fuck Michael,* I thought, shocking myself.

"My sister was right," I mumbled. "There will be plenty more." She was always telling me that Michael wasn't the only one.

"Huh?" Gabriel said.

"Nothing," I said. "You can take your time with the car. Can I watch?"

"Whatever," he said, shrugging. But I caught him looking back over his shoulder at me, checking me out.

I slid off the stool and followed him out into the sunlight.

Shelly Stoehr

"One other thing," I said, "could you disconnect the tape player? It's been driving me crazy."

"You'll probably lose that tape in there," he said.

"It's okay," I said. "It's old, and I'd like to hear something new from now on."

I'd miss the troll bumps, but it would be cool to see what magical things would show up if I started dreaming my own dreams again. Watching Gabriel's feet sticking out from under the Nova, I was pretty sure I'd be dreaming of holey Converse sneakers tonight.

about "Troll Bumps"

Several years ago I moved cross-country to California from New York, and that voyage inspired the cross-country trip of Grace in my story, "Troll Bumps." One night, about halfway through my trip, I remember stopping for the night in Iowa City. The air was fresh, the grass was green, and rabbits were hopping around in people's front yards—it was so very different from anywhere I'd ever lived! As I explored the area in the early evening, actually eating ribs in a place called Porky's, as Grace does in the story, I wondered what it would be like if I just stopped traveling and settled down, right there in Iowa. Being a city girl, as well as a coastal girl who needed a regular dose of the ocean, I was scared half to death by the thought—but it also intrigued me.

The rest of the inspiration for "Troll Bumps" came later, after I'd already been living in northern California for a few years, when I met a guy from L.A. and started thinking about moving south.

Although Grace is still a teenager, and it seems so typical of "young love" that she would up and take off after her dream guy, Michael, in fact I believe it is typical of many women of *all* ages to drop everything and move—even great distances, even at great personal risk and with precious little forethought—for the sake of love. I've seen this tendency in my sister, in my female friends, and in the female partners of some of my male friends. Maybe it is the teenager in all of us.

In the end, the relationship with my "Michael" was short and not so dreamy as I'd first thought. But you know, I still moved south to Los Angeles! It was just for a different guy—not at all unlike Grace, who will probably stay in Iowa after all. . . .

Shelly Stoehr

about Shelley Stoehr

Shelley Stoehr is the author of four acclaimed novels for young adults: *Crosses* (which was published when she was still a student at Connecticut College), *Weird on the Outside, Wannabe,* and *Tomorrow Wendy. Crosses* was an American Library Association Best Book for Young Adults, a Quick Pick for Reluctant Young Adult Readers, and a 1999 Popular Paperback for Young Adults. Hailed as "one of the new young breed of truth-telling young adult writers," she has been a guest on the Maury Povich television show and on numerous radio programs as an expert on teen self-injuring, or "cutting," the subject of *Crosses.*

Shelley Stoehr lives in southern California with her husband, Chris, and her two dogs, Bone and Max.

It rained the night I started following and watching Jacks.

Watcher

by Angela Johnson

Merriam-Webster's defines obsession as: a persistent disturbing preoccupation with an often unreasonable idea or feeling; compelling motivation.

I used to hang around Public Square and watch the cars almost run one another off the street. If not there then the library off of East Ninth. I could spend a whole day there just wandering around. Room to room. Scuffing along the marble floors. I used to lose myself—alone in the city.

Mostly I would people-watch.

Jacks talks about how she once almost got locked in the library; and Ruth asks her if she could find anything—just anything at all—to do in the city of Cleveland other than almost getting locked in libraries.

She did.

She followed me. It all started with obsession, you see. The first time was in the Arcade. I was in a jewelry store with my sister on the first floor, and Jacks was watching me from a railing on the second.

She says there was something about me that moved her. She says it was the way I leaned my head to the side to talk to my sister.

The second thing that got her was my hands. When I walked out of the shop, I held up the necklace my sister had bought to the light above us. The hands did it. And she had to know me. . . .

The way Jacks talks about following me, you'd think she was some kind of stalker. She says maybe she was, but she says people are too strange not to take an interest in. Jacks is a watcher, and I would be one soon too.

I told her not to tell people about it though.

You know, there're just some things . . .

Jacks lives downtown with her godmother, Ruth, on the top floor of a building. They have a roof garden that Jacks's been watching people from since she was four.

I can almost see her then. Ponytails blowing in the wind—her on tiptoes as she looks down on all of it. The city. The people.

I can see her now. Her dreads blowing over the railings, her looking down on Euclid Avenue, and me watching her.

Some days when I'm alone I dream that I can touch her, feel how the room changes when she walks through it. When Jacks walks toward me, I almost pass out sometimes. Man, that isn't something you go around telling your posse.

But sometimes I want to tell everybody. Scream it out . . . run down the street shouting like they do at the church down the street.

She is my religious experience.

Jacks isn't what most people call beautiful, but there is

Angela Johnson

no doubt I think she's the finest person in the world. My sister says sometimes we burn up a room looking at each other—and what with Jacks four inches taller than me, we stick out.

What do they know about the sensual her? They couldn't ever have touched her like I do. I know every part of her, every part.

How could anybody call my Jacks, with the long arms and legs that swing in rhythm to her own private music, strange.

They know nothing.

I know though.

My bones know it. I know it the way she looks at me in the hall at school. I know it the way she closes the car door and stands looking at me while I'm deciding if I should leave and go home, or not.

Used to ache at night for Jacks, and I thought something was wrong with me. I mean, it wasn't just my body that ached. It was my heart. Yeah, it was my heart, and I ain't afraid of saying it. But at first I thought it was just my body.

I grew up in a house where my mom said it was okay to touch yourself in private, and to hell with those self-righteous idiots who talked about going to hell but did the same thing when they could.

That wasn't a problem.

It's only when I started dreaming of Jacks and waking up in tears that I knew something was wrong. It was only when I started calling her name out in my sleep and not eating, I knew she was in me. I knew too that there was a part of Jacks that would never leave me.

Never.

I wouldn't let her.

"You gonna eat those fries, or what?"

I look across the booth at Jacks and then down at the chili fries that are about to congeal. I push the plate across to her.

"No, you can have them."

She starts sucking the fries down like she hasn't eaten in a week. She always eats like that. I'm used to it. Count on it, even. Her lips move slowly. She gets all the taste out of the fries before she swallows them.

I say, "You want some more?"

She says, "Yeah, I do," then reaches under the table and grabs my knee. I hold on to her hand while she keeps eating her chili fries. By the time she's done, it's raining, and I don't want to leave The Diner to go out into it.

Jacks writes her name, then mine, on the fogged-up window beside her. She has to write with her right hand 'cause I have her left one, still caressing it under the table.

Jacks never knew her parents. They were dead and she was in foster homes by the time she was one. She says she has dreams that she remembers them. She says that sometimes she wakes up and swears that they're sitting on her bed.

Jacks says the only time she thinks about her parents is

at night. She says she can see them only in the dark. It worries me.

Even though Jacks is always surrounded by people, I think she's lonely. I think that's why she watches. She can get only so far out of her loneliness. Sometimes when she falls asleep on my couch, she seems like the loneliest person I ever met. When she looks like that, I rub her back while she sleeps—which always wakes her up and makes me not see her loneliness.

I like the feel of our bare skin next to each other as we lie shirtless. Her, milk-chocolate brown as she glows in the soft light, and me pale as a mutant who needs iron. And just as I'm about to fall deep into sleep, she watches me, looking deep down and not letting me feel alone like her.

Jacks got it in her mind when she was six that her parents weren't dead but were living on her block off Euclid Avenue.

She started following people in her building first. When the laundry room was full on Saturdays, she'd go down there to pick out her parents. She says she'd follow the people who smiled at her. Then she'd watch them from that day on.

Since she lived on the top floor, she watched the world.

The first time Jacks and me made love, I don't think that I breathed the whole time. It wasn't 'cause I thought we'd be caught or anything—Ruth was gone for the weekend. I held my breath because I knew I was going to die.

Watcher

Most people get spared that feeling. I don't remember how her face looked as we started kissing by the door. We almost fell into a gigantic aloe plant that Jacks had been growing since she was little.

I remember how her neck tasted as I ran my tongue slowly, so slowly, from the front of it to the back.

I remember that when we were finally lying down on the big, soft couch, I thought I'd melt into her—and she into me.

It wasn't anything like what my running buddies—who claimed to have done it a hundred times—with a thousand girls—told me it would be.

There wasn't anyone else in the world but me and her. After a while I didn't know where her body stopped and mine started. I didn't know if I was doing it right. How would I know?

How would she know?

We were stumbling and touching each other in a cloud, with the sun just burning up the city. And I was thinking that I could just die, lying across her smooth skin as long as she would let me.

It's okay that we didn't know anything, because it was okay to make it up as we went.

What I couldn't believe was the softness. She was so soft and so giving; I gave too.

Jacks told me later that she always thought it was so cool how we fit each other's body. She said I fit perfectly— walking beside her, kissing her, making love.

It used to embarrass me when she'd talk about sex when

we had our clothes on. She'd say I should get over it, and I'm trying to. I'm afraid of talking about it, 'cause I still lose control when I see her walking, even. There've been a couple of rough moments at school when I couldn't stand up or had to cover up with a book. She moves me, and there is no doubt about it. None.

Me and Jacks could sit up on the roof and talk about everything.

We walk around downtown in the evening and look at old buildings, not noticing anybody in the whole world. I would hold my breath then, too, because sometimes when Jacks would laugh or put her hand in mine and brush against me, I worried that none of what I am feeling could be real.

It's too good.

My grandparents are serious Christians who think that if it feels too good, you probably shouldn't be doing it. And that includes food and movies. My mom raised me opposite.

That's why I think it's so good for me and Jacks. She's always looking for something that will make her feel good. She says that if you do it right, you can make it an art form (feeling good). You can just set your time aside and watch life as a big pleasure palace.

She says you don't have to be selfish about it or hurt other people when you're going in search of pleasure. You just have to get it straight in your mind that you can make all the world yours. If you do it right. . . .

Watcher

And we do.

That's why I watch her.

It rained all night the day before I started following and watching Jacks.

I guess it sounds stupid to follow someone you could be with most anytime you want. I have to explain that part. I mean, that part is important and I don't want anybody to get the wrong idea. I know everyone will anyway—but I have to try.

Most people who follow other people around secretly have been told to stay away from the person. It's not like that with me and Jacks.

I follow her because I want all of her in different ways. Not just walking along with each other or eating greasy fries at The Diner. I want to have her time when she thinks she's having it alone. . . . I want to be there with her when she sleeps, eats, and cries.

I'm not a dangerous stalker. Watching Jacks (and she knows I do it) is passion. It's very safe sex, watching and wanting.

One night it rained so hard we laid in front of the TV, not really watching anything. Jacks got up to look out the window, pressing her face into the rainy night sky.

For a few minutes she went away from me, and I almost cried because I didn't ever remember her doing that before. I thought she knew something that I should know.

Angela Johnson

I went to her, standing behind her, rubbing her stomach. My touch didn't bring her back fast enough. I felt her slipping away. But slowly she came back to me, and the sky exploded with lightning.

That was the first time I had to have all of her.

The second time was the next day, when I followed her through the steamy streets of Cleveland. Following and wanting her. Wanting and following her.

Through the streets, in and out of stores, I follow her now, my heart stopping when she stops to talk to people I don't know—want to know because they know her.

I want to know all she knows. It's almost like I want to be in her skin. Walk around in it and be her for a while. It was scary for a while. But now that's just how it is.

I don't know how it could ever not be this way. Me and Jacks. Jacks and me. Me watching Jacks, and Jacks knowing, seeing me watch her. Enjoying my eyes on her as she goes about it all.

I'm a watcher of Jacqueline.

It is more sensual than skin to skin, body to body, lips to lips.

I watch her as she tries on boots (on Prospect Avenue) and buys pretzels from a vendor that she laughs with—but then, with one quick turn, loses herself and me in the city.

about "Watcher"

I've often wondered about the intensity of adolescent love and, so, the lengths to which it drives young people.

As there is nothing like first love, what about a first love and a first sexual encounter all rolled into one? Just how intense can these feelings become, since adolescence is a time of thoroughly intense *everything*, including love in its most heightened form, powerful and sensual.

Obsession is a strong word but apt in situations of overwhelming want and overpowering attraction. Yet, in the end "Watcher" is about a love between two young people that may not be conventional but is love, nonetheless.

Angela Johnson

about Angela Johnson

Angela Johnson is a novelist, poet, and picture book author, whose work for young adults includes the novels *Toning the Sweep, Humming Whispers, Songs of Faith,* and *Heaven.* She is also the author of *The Other Side,* a work of poetry, and *Gone from Home,* a short-story collection. Born in Alabama, she grew up in Ohio, but family ties to the South inspire her work, which has received many honors and awards, including the Ezra Jack Keats Award, the Coretta Scott King Award (twice), the PEN America/Norma Klein Award, and the Lee Bennett Hopkins Poetry Award.

Angela Johnson lives in Ohio, close to her family.

I was sad then, and Di could tell.

"Don't worry about it, Luce," she said gently, shoveling the chopped carrots into the pot. "In the long run, you know, if two people matter to each other, it doesn't make much difference whether they've ever actually done the business or not."

She meant her and me, but in the weeks that followed I tried applying her words to me and J. J. I repeated them to myself whenever J. J. left the room. If it was love, it should be enough on its own.

The Welcome

by Emma Donoghue

Women's Housing Coop Seeks Member. Low Rent, Central Manchester. Applicants Must Have Ability to Get On With People and Show Comittment To Cooperative Living. All Ethnic Backgrounds Particularly Welcome To Apply.

I tore stripes off Carola when I noticed that ad, taped up in the window of the newsagent's next door to our house. She said I could hardly complain, if I'd missed the meeting where the wording of the ad was agreed on, but I should feel free to share my feelings with the Policy Group anyway. "They're not feelings," I said, "they're facts."

Dear Policy Group, I typed furiously. *Re: Recruitment Ad. I suggest we use a hyphen in* co-op, *if we don't want the Welcome Cooperative to be confused with a chicken coop. Some other problems with this ad: "Seeks member" sounds like we don't have any members yet. Do you mean "seeks new member"? And besides, it sounds rather like a giant dildo. Also, I'm just curious, why should the applicants HAVE "ability to get on with people" (and is* People *a euphemism for* women, *by the way, given that this is a women-only co-op?), but only SHOW "commitment to cooperative living" (commitment being spelled with two m's and one* t, *not vice versa, by the way, in case anyone cares)? Or are you suggesting that an applicant might claim to HAVE such a commitment but needs to be forced to SHOW it (e.g., through housework)? And if so, why not say so?*

The way I see it, there's not much point having policies on equal opportunities and accessibility and class and race issues if we're going to keep on writing our ads in politically correct gobbledygook that would put off anyone who's not doing a Ph.D. And speaking of race issues, what on earth does it mean to say that "ALL ethnic backgrounds" ("members of all ethnic groups," I think you mean) are "particularly welcome to apply"? Who's not so particularly welcome, then? Or do you mean white people don't count as an ethnic group? I can't believe one four-line ad can give such an impression of confusion, illiteracy, and pomposity all at once. Why can't we just say what we mean?

My hands were shaking, so I left it at that and printed out the page. *Yours, Luce,* I'd added at the bottom, as if it weren't totally obvious from vocabulary alone who'd written the letter. As Di was always telling me, "It's like you've got the Oxford English Dictionary hidden up your arse." She had a point; some days I sounded more like eighty than eighteen. I suppose I'd read too many books to be normal.

It was only when I was sealing the letter into the envelope that I remembered: In my absence at the last co-op meeting they'd decided to rotate me from the maintenance crew to the Policy Group because, as I'd been pointing out for years, my syntax was a lot better than my plumbing. I was meant to replace Nuala, who was moving back to Cork,

Emma Donoghue

and if Rachel made up her mind to go off for three months to that organic farm in Cornwall, it occurred to me now, there'd be no one left in the Policy Group but myself and Di, and I'd end up handing her my letter like some mad silent protester. Or if Di happened to be away that evening, on one of those Buddhist retreats her boyfriend ran, it would be just me having a one-person meeting, and I'd have to read my own letter aloud and make snide comments about it.

Arghhhh. The joys of communal living. After two years in the Welcome Co-op I could hardly remember living any other way.

I ripped the envelope open and went downstairs. In the kitchen I pinned my letter up on the corkboard over the oven—the only place you could be sure everyone would see it. I went back down for a prawn cracker five minutes later and found Di reading it as she stirred her miso. "The ad was appalling," I said defensively.

"Yeah. Carola wrote it after the rest of us had gone down to the pub. You know you use the word *mean* four times in the last paragraph?" she asked, grinning.

I ripped the thing down and stuffed it into the recycling bin.

"Temper, temper," she said, tucking away a pale curl that had come out of her bun.

I licked my prawn cracker. "What's wrong with me these days, Di?"

"You know what's wrong with you."

"Apart from that." I shifted uncomfortably against the wooden counter.

"There is no apart from that, Luce. You've been a virgin too long."

My head was hammering; I rubbed the stiff muscles at the back of my neck. "Why does every conversation in this house have to come back to the same old, same old?"

"Well, Jesus, child, take a look at yourself."

I glanced down as if I'd gotten food on my shirt.

"You came out at fifteen, but you haven't done a thing about it yet. For years now you've seen every kind of woman pass through these doors, and you haven't let one of them lay a hand on you. No wonder you've got a headache!"

I was out the door and halfway through the garden by then. Di was fabulous, but I could do without another of her rants about regular orgasms being crucial to health. Nurses were all like that.

The June sun was slipping behind the crab-apple tree. My zucchini were beginning to flower, a wonderful pale orange. I picked a couple of insects off them. When I moved into the Welcome the week after my sixteenth birthday—so my mother would have had no legal way of dragging me back home, if she'd tried, not that she did—anyway, at first I'd found the constant company unbearable. I'd been used to spending all my after-school time locked in my bedroom with a book, living in the world of the Brontës or Jung or Isabel Allende, just about any world would do, so long as it wasn't the one my mother lived in. And now all at once I was supposed to become part of some bizarre nine-woman feminist family. The housing co-op was what I'd chosen, but it freaked me out all the same. In the early weeks digging the garden was the only thing that kept me halfway sane. The vegetable plot had been strictly organic ever since I took it over, but sometimes I got the impression that most of my sweat went into providing a feast for the crawlies.

Di was sort of right. I was a pedant, a twitching spinster, dried up before my time, and I'd only just finished secondary school! Sixty-seven fortnightly co-op meetings (I'd counted them up recently) had frayed me to a thread: all those good intentions, all that mind-numbingly imprecise jargon. These days even typos in the *Guardian* made me itch. When I was old, I knew I wouldn't wear purple, like in the poem; instead I'd limp around under cover of darkness, correcting the punctuation on billboards with a spray can. Rachel said I should become a proofreader and make a mint, instead of starting political studies at the university this October and probably ending up politically somewhere to the right of Baroness Thatcher. On my eighteenth birthday, when Di gave me a T-shirt that read DOES ANAL RETENTIVE HAVE A HYPHEN?, I was too busy considering the question to get the joke.

It wasn't that I didn't like the idea of sex, by the way. I was just picky. And somehow, the more free-floating fornication that went on in the Welcome—the louder the shrieks from Carola's attic room, the more often I walked into the living room and found anonymous bodies pillowing the sofa—the less I felt like attempting it. Besides, there was never enough privacy. At my birthday party I got as far as kissing a German acupuncturist, and by breakfast the next morning my housemates had given me: (a) a pack of latex gloves (Di), (b) much conflicting advice about sexual positions (Rachel, Maura, Iona, and the two Londoners whose names I was always getting the wrong way around), and (c) a paperback called *Safe Space: Coping with Issues Around Intimacy* (Carola, of course). The acupuncturist left me a message, but I never rang back. Collectively my housemates had managed to put me right off.

So Nuala went back to Cork, and that's how it all began. The Welcome's rent was so low it was never hard to fill a place. We interviewed seven women one endless, hot Saturday at the end of June. I was the one who volunteered to tell J. J. she was the lucky winner.

"I wasn't sure it was all right to ring at nearly midnight," I told her on the phone.

"Yeah, no problem. That's . . . excellent." Her voice was as deep as Tracy Chapman's and hoarse with excitement.

"Well, we're all really glad," I added, somehow not wanting the call to be over so soon.

I could hear J. J. let out a long breath of relief. "I never thought I'd hear from you people again, actually. I made such a cock-up of the interview."

"Not at all!" I said, laughing too loudly.

"But I hardly said a word."

"Well, we figured you were just shy, you know. All the others were brash young things who got on our nerves."

Di, passing through with a tray of margaritas for her hospital friends, who were partying on the balcony, raised one eyebrow.

It was kind of a lie; we hadn't been at all unanimous. Carola had voted for a ghastly woman from Leeds who claimed to be very vulnerable after a series of relationships with emotionally abusive men and wanted to know did we do co-counseling after house meetings? But in the end I played the race card, like the hypocrite I was; I told Carola that if we were serious about particularly welcoming and all that—if we wanted to improve the co-op's representation of women of color from none in nine to one in nine—then we had to pick J. J.

Not that her being black had anything to do with it for me. I wanted J. J. because her fingers were long and broad and made me feel slightly shaky.

The day she was to move in, I came downstairs to find the living room transformed. There was a Mexican blanket slung over the back of the pink couch and an African head scarf wrapped around the lamp shade, and my framed print of Gertrude Stein appeared to have metamorphosed into a dog-eared poster of a woman carrying a stack of bricks on her head that said OXFAM IN INDIA: EMPOWERMENT THROUGH EDUCATION.

Rachel, Di, and Iona claimed to know nothing about the changes. Carola said she was only acting on the advice of a book called *Antiracism for Housing Co-ops*. She was trying to make the atmosphere more inclusive, less Anglo-Saxon.

"Gertrude Stein was an American Jew!" I protested.

"She lived on inherited wealth," said Carola, spooning up her porridge.

"So?"

"So I just don't think we should cover our walls with images of women of privilege; it sends out the wrong signals."

"Gertrude Stein covered only about three square feet of the wall!"

Carola rolled her pale blue eyes. "You're being petty, Luce. I wonder why you've got so much invested in the status quo?"

"Because the status quo was a pretty stylish living room. And you know what signals this room is sending out now, Carola? Embarrassingly obvious, geographically muddled white-guilt signals!"

She pointed out that we all had feelings around these issues.

"Feelings about," I corrected her, "not around, about," and it all went downhill from there, especially when I pulled down the Oxfam poster and a corner tore off. Di had to intervene, and it took hours of "feelings around" before we reached a grudging compromise: yes to the Mexican blanket, no to the lamp shade wrap, and okay to a laminated poster of dolphins that none of us liked.

I'd been planning to do some weeding that afternoon because my eyes were sore from reading Dostoyevsky in a Victorian edition with tiny print, but I was afraid I wouldn't hear the front door. I pottered around in my room instead, and when I heard the bell, I ran downstairs to help J. J. carry up her stuff. But she didn't have much in the way of stuff, it turned out: two backpacks, a duvet, and a rat.

I backed away from the cage.

"Ah, yeah, his name's Victor," she said nervously, clearing her throat. "I forgot to mention him at the interview."

"Oh, I'm sure everyone'll love him," I told her, grabbing the cage by its handle and frantically thinking, *hamster, it's more or less a hamster*. I managed to carry the cage all the way upstairs without looking inside.

I was going to offer to help J. J. unpack, but somehow I lost my nerve. There was something private about the way she dropped her bags in the corner beside Victor's cage and stood looking out the window. "This room gets the sun in the late afternoon," I told her. "I lived here my first year in the co-op." But she just nodded and smiled a little, without looking back at me.

That night we had a communal dinner in J. J.'s honor, even though when the nine of us sat down together, there was barely elbow room to use a fork. I talked too much, ate too much of Melissa's sushi and Kay's gooseberry fool, and felt rather ill. J. J. seemed to listen attentively to the conversation—which covered global warming, how to eat a litchi, the government's treachery, what we wanted done with our bodies when we died, and (the inevitable topic) female ejaculation—but she said even less than she had at her interview, though I wouldn't have thought that was possible. I wondered whether we sounded peculiar to her, or ranty, or Anglo-Saxon.

Iona carried in the tray of coffee, chai, chamomile tea, and soy shake. "So tell us, J. J.," said Carola with a sympathetic smile, "is it going to make you feel at all uncomfortable, d'you think, being the only woman of color in the co-op?"

Di rolled her eyes at me, but it was too awful to be funny. I stared out the window at my tomato plants, mortified.

But J. J. just shrugged and sipped her coffee.

Carola wouldn't let it rest, of course. "How old would you say you were, like, when you first became aware of systemic racism?"

"Carola!" Di and I groaned in unison.

This time J. J. let out a little grunt that could have been the beginning of a laugh. Then she muttered something that sounded like "Bodies are an accident."

If I hadn't been sitting right beside her, I mightn't have caught that at all. Startled, I looked down at myself. A short, skinny, pale, postadolescent Anglo-Saxon body; a random conglomeration of genes.

Afterward J. J. volunteered to wash up, so I said she and I would do it and everybody else was to get out of the kitchen. Some went to bed and some went out to smoke dope by the bonfire, and I got to stand beside J. J., watching how gently she handled the plates. I took them dripping from her big hands, one by one, and wiped them dry.

Her hundreds of skinny plaits gleamed; I wondered how

Emma Donoghue

she kept them like that. Under her army surplus shirt her shoulders were wider that anyone's I knew. She had all she needed to be a total butch and didn't seem to realize it.

"So how did you pick the name?" she asked at last, jerking me out of my daze.

"What—Luce? Well, I was christened Lucy, but I've always—"

"No," she interrupted softly, "the co-op's name, the Welcome."

"Oh," I said with an embarrassed laugh.

"Is it, like, meant to sound like everyone's welcome?"

"No, actually, it's named after some defunct co-op down in London, on Welcome Street," I told her. "When they folded, they passed the leftover money to a group in Manchester that was just starting up. Before my time."

"So are you really only eighteen?"

I almost blushed as I nodded.

J. J. had to be in her twenties herself, but she didn't specify. In fact, she hadn't volunteered any information about herself yet, it occurred to me now.

The whole time I'd lived in the Welcome—with all the guff that got talked about *acceptance* and *non-judgmentalism*—I'd never met anyone half as accepting as J. J. Her tolerance even crossed the species barrier; it didn't seem to have occurred to her, for instance, that a rat wasn't a suitable pet. (And Victor did turn out to be a total charmer.) Like a visitor from Mars, J. J. displayed no fixed opinions about race, class, or any other label. Though she'd chosen to live in a women-only housing co-op, I never heard her make a single generalization about men (unlike, say, Iona, whose favorite joke that summer was "What's the best way to make a man come? Who the fuck cares!").

When various housemates talked as if all the world were queer, J. J. didn't join in, but she didn't make any objection, either. She listened with her head bent, wearing what Di called her "wary Bambi" look. At J. J.'s interview, I remembered, it was Rachel who'd come out with the usual uncomfortable spiel about "This co-op has members of a variety of sexualities," and instead of giving either of the two usual responses—"Oh, but I have a boyfriend" or "Fab!"—J. J. had just nodded, eyes elsewhere, as if she were being told how the washing machine worked.

Shy people annoyed Di; she thought it was too much hard work digging conversation out of them, and the results were rarely worth it.

"But is she or isn't she, though?" I begged Di.

"How should I know, Luce?"

"Didn't they teach you how to assess people at nursing school?"

Di laughed and flicked her hair back from her soup bowl. She blew on her spoon before she answered me. "Only their health. All I can tell you is the woman seems in good shape, apart from a bit of acne and a few stone she could afford to lose."

I felt mildly offended by that—J. J. being the perfect

Emma Donoghue

shape, in my book—but I stuck to the point. "Yeah, but is she a dyke?"

Di twinkled at me. "What do you care, Miss Celibate?"

Not that I thought I had much of a chance, whatever kind of sexuality the woman had, but I needed to know anyway. Just to have some information on J. J. Just to find out whether it was worth letting her into my dreams.

One evening when I came in after the news, J. J. told me, "The government are cutting housing benefits" and before I could stop myself, I said, "The government *is*."

Her thick black eyebrows contracted.

"Sorry. It's just—"

"Yeah?"

"It's a collective noun," I muttered, mortified. "It takes the singular. But it doesn't matter." I suddenly heard myself: What an unbearably tedious teenager!

But J. J.'s bright teeth widened into a grin. "You like to classify things, don't you, Luce?" she said. "Everything in its little box."

"I suppose so." I thought about how good my name sounded in her husky voice.

"Do you classify people too?"

"Sometimes," I said, trying to sound cheeky now, rather than obnoxious. "Like you, for instance, I'd say . . ." I was bluffing; I tried to think of something she'd like to hear. "I'd say you're someone who's at peace with herself, I suppose," I told her. "Because you speak only when you've something to say. Unlike someone like me, who rabbits on and on and on all the time." I shut my mouth then and covered it with my hand.

The light was behind J. J.; I couldn't read her eyes. "That's how you'd describe me, is it, Luce? At peace with myself?"

"Yeah," I said doubtfully.

She put her throat back and roared. Her deep laughter filled the room.

"What's the joke?" asked Rachel, sticking her head in the door, but I just shrugged.

Well, at least J. J. found me funny, I told myself. It was better than nothing.

I still hadn't gathered a single clue about her sexual orientation. Some mornings I woke with the clenched face that told me I'd been grinding my teeth again. To me, the fact that I was a dyke had been clear as glass by my thirteenth birthday, but then, precision was my thing. Maybe J. J. was one too and didn't know it yet, would never know it till my kiss woke her. Or maybe she was one of those "labels are for clothes" people, who couldn't bear to be categorized. She dressed like a truck driver, but so did half the straight girls nowadays. With anyone else I would have pumped her friends for information, but J. J. didn't seem to have any friends in Manchester. She worked long shifts at the Pizza Palace, and she never brought anyone home.

We got on best, I found, when we just talked about day-to-day matters like the color of the sky. No big questions, no heavy issues. The sweetest times that summer were when she came out to help me with the vegetables. After a long July day we'd each take a hose and water one side of the garden, not speaking till we met at the end by the crabapple tree. Sometimes she brought Victor's cage down from her room for an airing. If Iona—who called him "that rodent"—wasn't in the garden, J. J. would let him out for a run; once I even fed him a crumb from my hand.

We got talking about why I wanted to do politics at college in the autumn. "I just think it'll be interesting to find out how things work," I said.

"What things?"

"Big things," I said, trying to sound dry and witty. "Countries, information systems, the global economy, that sort of thing. What goes on and why."

J. J. shook her head as if marveling and bent down to rip up some bindweed. I waited to hear what she thought; you couldn't rush her. "I dunno," she said at last, "I find it hard enough to understand what's going on inside me."

I waited as I trained the hose on the tomato patch, but she didn't say another word.

Some days that summer I had this peculiar sense of waiting, from when I first rolled out of my single bed till long after midnight, when I switched off my light; my stomach was tight with it. But nothing momentous ever happened. J. J. never told me what I was waiting to hear—whatever that was.

She lavished care on Victor the rat, stroking his coat and scratching behind his ears with a methodical tenderness that softened me like candle wax. But she never touched another human being, that I could see. She wouldn't take or give massages; instead of good-bye hugs, she nodded at people. It was just how J. J. was. I knew I shouldn't take it personally, but of course I did.

Iona didn't like her one bit, I could tell. Iona specialized in having enough information to take the piss out of anyone; pinned to her bedroom wall was a sprawling multicolored diagram of who'd shagged whom on the Manchester women's scene since 1990. One evening a few of us were in the living room, and J. J. was stroking Victor all the way down his spine with one finger, very slowly and firmly. Iona walked in and said "I get it! You don't fancy humans at all, just rats."

J. J. threw Iona one unreadable look, scooped Victor back into his cage, and disappeared up the stairs.

The room was silent. "Aren't you ever going to give up?" I asked, without looking up from my book.

"Oh, she's probably just another repressed virgin," Iona threw in my direction.

But it didn't even have to be comments about sex that made J. J. bolt, I discovered. She was prickly about the slightest things. For instance, one Sunday morning most of us were lying around in the garden, half naked. J. J. was wrapped up in her huge white flannel dressing gown, as usual. Rachel, bored of the newspaper, started teasing me about waxing my mustache off.

"What are you talking about?" I said.

"I saw your little box of wax strips in the bathroom,

Luce. Trying to get all respectable before you start college, are you?"

J. J. lurched out of her deck chair so fast she knocked it over. She stomped off into the house, her dressing gown enveloping her like a ghostly monk's robe. We all stared at one another.

"Which particular sore point was that?" snapped Rachel.

I shrugged uncertainly. "Maybe the wax is hers."

"Who cares if it is?" Iona butted in. "I've got pubes down to my knees, for god's sake!"

Di spoke from behind her magazine. "Hands up who didn't need to know that."

Di, Kay, and I put our hands in the air. Maura let out a yelp of laughter.

"Well, one reason I moved in here," growled Iona, "was to get away from that crap about what should and shouldn't be talked about. Nothing's unmentionable!"

"Yeah, well, you can mention what you like as long as you leave J. J. alone." That came out more loudly than I meant it to. I kept my eyes on the article on permaculture I was skimming. In the silence I could almost hear the others exchange amused glances. Nothing was ever private in the Welcome.

It troubled me that J. J. would be so embarrassed about something petty like having a slight, faint mustache. Hadn't anybody ever told her what a handsome face she had? Now I came to think about it, she couldn't bear praise. "*Seriously* cute," I'd let myself say once when she came in wearing a new pair of combat trousers—that was all, two words—and she glanced down as if she'd never seen herself before and froze up. Could it be that she didn't like her body—the solid, glorious bulk that I let myself think of only last thing at night, in the dark?

Di was doing the pressure points in my neck one night during the news; she said I felt like old rope.

"Sleek and flexible?"

"No, all hard with salt and knotted round itself."

I stared glumly at the TV pictures from the Balkans.

"Jesus, Luce," said Di out of nowhere, "why her?"

My head whipped around.

Di pushed it back into place gently. "And don't say, 'who?' You're so obvious. Whenever J. J.'s in the room, you sit with your limbs sort of *parted* at her."

My face scalded. "No, I don't."

"Even Kay's noticed, and Kay wouldn't register the fall of a nuclear bomb."

I hid my face in my hand.

"Of all people to fall for!" said Di crossly.

"What's wrong with her?" I asked.

"J. J.'s an untouchable, honey."

I flinched at the word.

"You know it's true. That rat is the only one let into her bed. You'll never get anywhere with her in a million years. Don't take it personally; nobody could get past that force field."

"I think she cares about me," I said, very low. "When I

had bad cramps last month," I added in what I knew was a pathetic voice, "she left a tulip outside my door."

"Of course she cares about you," said Di pityingly. "Leave it at that."

But she didn't know how it was. J. J. and I stayed up late sometimes, after the others had all gone to bed; we raided the fruit bowl and watched any old rubbish that was on television. Once, in the middle of a rerun of *Some Like It Hot*, my hand was lying on the couch about half an inch from hers, but no matter what I told myself, I couldn't bring myself to close the gap. J. J. stared at the flickering screen, quite unaware.

I couldn't sleep too many nights like that one, wondering what it would be like. Just the back of her hand against mine, that's all I imagined. I had a feeling it would be hot enough to burn.

August came in hot and cloudy. The tomatoes hung fat but green in the humid garden. Di and I were peeling carrots one morning. She was looking baggy eyed after a bad shift in the emergency room. "Your problem is, Luce,"—she began out of nowhere—"you're too picky. You'll never find everything you're looking for in one woman."

"What if I already have?" I muttered, mutinous.

She let out a heavy sigh to show what she thought of that.

I knew I shouldn't push it, but I couldn't stop. "What if J. J.'s my ideal woman?"

"Your ideal fantasy, you mean. Listen, next time try picking someone who's willing to sleep with you. Call me old-fashioned, but it's a big plus!"

Irritated, I gave my finger a bad scrape with the peeler.

"You should have copped off with someone your first week in this house," said Di.

"With whom, exactly?" I asked, sucking the blood off my knuckle.

"I don't know," she said, "someone old and wise and relaxed who wouldn't have put you through any of this angst. Someone like me," she added, lopping off a carrot top.

I stared at her through my sweaty fringe. "You're not serious," I told her.

"Well, no," said Di with one of her dirty laughs. There was a pause. "But I might have been, two years ago," she added lightly, "when you were all fresh and tempting."

"It's a bit bloody late to tell me now!" My voice was shrill with confusion.

"Oh, chop your carrots, child."

We worked on. I thought about Di and about her current boyfriend, Theo, quite a witty guy who remembered to put the seat down and seemed to have more staying power than her others—judging by the retreats he ran, which involved sitting cross-legged on a mat for six hours a day and "understanding the pain," apparently. "Besides," I said at last, getting my thoughts in order, "you're straight."

She laughed again and did her *Star Trek* voice. "Classification error alert!"

I was sad, then, and Di could tell.

Emma Donoghue

"Don't worry about it, Luce," she said gently, shoveling the chopped carrots into the pot. "In the long run, you know, if two people matter to each other, it doesn't make much difference whether they've ever actually done the business or not."

She meant her and me, but in the weeks that followed I tried applying her words to me and J. J. I repeated them to myself whenever J. J. left the room. If it was love, it should be enough on its own.

On the August bank holiday the weather was so sticky I felt like my skin was crawling. It was too unpleasant to work in the garden, even. J. J. was at the Pizza Palace all day; I just hoped they were paying her time and a half. I sat in the shady living room and did a cryptic crossword with 108 clues. Whenever any of the others wandered by, they offered to help, but they only gave stupid answers.

At ten that evening Carola came downstairs to watch some grim documentary about child abuse. I kept on struggling with the crossword. J. J. walked in at half past ten, limp, with her uniform still on. I offered her cold mint tea from my herb patch; she grinned and said she'd love some, after her shower. I decided it was going to be a good night after all.

It still would have been, if Iona hadn't been such a maladjusted bollocks. She and her latest, Lynn, were sitting around on the balcony drinking beer. They came downstairs just as J. J. was emerging from the bathroom, swaddled in her white dressing gown as usual. She looked cool and serene now; there were tiny flecks of water caught in her dreadlocks. She stood back against the wall to let Iona and Lynn go by; that was the kind of person she was, gentlemanly.

But Iona caught her by the lapel of her dressing gown and said "Hey, Lynn, have you met J. J.? She's the house prude!"

J. J. didn't smile. She just kept a tight hold of the neck of her thick robe.

Lynn was giggling, and Iona wouldn't leave it at that. She wasn't even drunk, she was just showing off. "Jesus, woman," she said in J. J.'s face, "how hot does it have to get before you'll show a little flesh?" She put on a parodic gymteacher voice: "We're all gells here, y'know!" As she spoke she hauled on the dressing gown and it fell open, and the next thing I knew, Iona was on the floor, clutching her face.

J. J., knotted into her robe again, had backed against the door.

"She hit me," howled Iona. "The bitch hit me in the eye!"

The next hour was the most awful I'd known in the Welcome. Rachel left her curry on high in the kitchen and ran in with the naturopathic first-aid kit. After dabbing Iona's eyelid with arnica, she wanted to take her off to the emergency room to have it checked out, "in case the co-op's legally liable," but Di told her not to be such a fuckwit. Every time one of the housemates came down to ask what all the noise was about this time of night, the story had to be told all

Emma Donoghue

over again, in its various competing versions. J. J. just sat on the edge of the couch with her face hidden in her hands, except when she was muttering "Sorry, I over-reacted, I'm so sorry," over and over again.

But Carola was the worst. It was as if for the five years she'd been attending co-op meetings and volunteering to go off to weekend workshops, she'd been in training for this. She got the policy book out of the kitchen drawer and read out clause 13 about "unreasonable and unacceptable behavior."

"*Behavior* means longer than half a second," I spit at her.

"Violence is unacceptable no matter how long it lasts," she said smoothly.

Kay burst into tears and said she'd come to this co-op to escape male aggression (which was the first any of us had heard of it). "I thought I'd be safe with women," she snuffled.

"You are safe," said Di coldly. "Nothing's happened to you. You were upstairs watering your plants till ten minutes ago."

"And besides," I said incoherently, "what about Iona's aggression? She started it. She tried to rip J. J.'s dressing gown off."

"I did not," growled Iona from behind the bag of frozen peas Lynn was holding to her face.

"You did so. You're the most aggressive person I've ever met, male or female," I bawled at her.

At which point Di tried to calm us all down. "Okay,

okay," she said, "let's agree that Iona . . . violated J. J.'s bodily integrity"—I could see her mouth twitch with laughter at the phrase—"and that J. J.—"

"Made a totally inappropriate response." Carola was icy.

"Oh, come on." I was pleading with her now. "Who's to say what's an appropriate response? These things happen. You can't make rules for everything."

But I was wrong, apparently. Carola had the policy book open to another page, and she was reading aloud. "'Step one, a formal letter of caution will be sent to Member B to instruct her to cease the offending behavior—'"

"She has ceased!" I looked over at J. J., who was bent over on the couch as if she had cramps.

"'—or not to repeat it.'"

There was a long pause. I drew breath. Well, who cared about a formal letter anyway? It would all blow over. We'd be laughing at this by next weekend.

"We don't know that she won't repeat the behavior," said Kay, quavering.

J. J. stood up then. Her hands hung heavy by her sides. "That's right," she said hoarsely, "you all don't know the first thing about anything."

The silence was broken by Carola, reading from the policy book again. "'In the case of an act of violence, the co-op may proceed directly to step three, eviction.'"

Everyone stared at her. None of us had noticed the smell till then, or the smoke fingering its way along the corridor. Only when the alarm began to squeal did we come to our

Emma Donoghue

senses.

In the kitchen the corkboard over Rachel's curry pot had gone up in flames. Di threw a bowl of water at it, putting out the fire and soaking Kay's pajamas. The smell was hideous. Phone messages, recycling schedules, minutes of meetings, a postcard from an ex-housemate in Java, and a pop-up card I'd gotten for my eighteenth birthday were all black and curled as feathers.

The eviction clause was never put to the test. J. J. gave in her notice the next day.

I was so full of rage I couldn't uncurl my fingers. "You could have stayed," I told her in her bedroom, not bothering to keep my voice down. "Why do the petty bureaucrats always have to win? It's Iona we should have kicked out, or Carola. All you did was defend yourself for half a second. Why is physical violence so much worse than the emotional kind, anyway?"

J. J. said nothing, just carrying on stowing away her rolled-up socks in the bottom of her backpack.

"My father hit my mother once," I told her, "and you know what?"

That made her look up.

"She deserved it. The things my mother used to say, I should have hit her myself." Now the tears were snaking down my face.

"Ah, Luce," said J. J. "Don't cry."

I sobbed like a child.

"I'd like to have stayed," she told me. "But I just don't

feel welcome anymore."

"You are! Welcome to me, anyway," I choked, ungrammatically.

J. J. came over to hug me then. I didn't quite believe she was going to do it. She hunched a little, as if her back was hurting her. She took me by the shoulders and warily laid her heavy head on my neck. I could feel her hot breath. She smelled of jasmine.

A mad idea came to me then. "Well, I'll move out too," I said brightly. "We can find a flat to share."

I could see her answer in her face even before she shook her head.

My ribs felt cold and leaden. "Where are you going, though? You don't have anywhere else to go. Listen, why don't I ring round some of the letting agencies for you? I've nearly a thousand pounds in my account. You can have it."

Her head kept gently swinging from side to side, saying no to everything. "I'll be okay," she whispered.

And then I saw in the back of her dark eyes that she did have somewhere to go, she just wasn't telling me. So I took a step backward and put my hands by my sides.

The taxi took her away. "Keep in touch," I shouted, a meaningless phrase because J. J. and I had never touched in our lives except for about five seconds, just before she left.

I didn't stay long at the Welcome myself, as it happened. Once I started college in the autumn, it seemed to make more sense to live in a student residence so I wouldn't have to trek across town.

The letter didn't reach me for months, because by then Di was off in Tibet and the others at the Welcome claimed to have mislaid my new address. I finally read it the day after Christmas, sitting on a park bench in the college grounds.

If I say hi, this is John, you won't know who I mean, will you? I used to think if anybody found me out, it would be you, Luce. Sometimes you used to look at me so intensely, like there was something on the tip of your tongue, I thought maybe you knew. But I was probably just kidding myself so I'd feel less guilty about bullshitting you all.

They said the hormones would be hard. But what I've found much worse is not quite belonging anywhere and having to lie all the time. Not that I ever had to actually claim to be a woman, because none of you ever asked.

And I am one, you know. Inside. Not where people usually mean by "inside," but further inside than that. I've known since I was four years old. I'm not John anymore, except on my birth certificate; I don't think I ever really was. I've been J. J. for a long time now. That's why it wasn't exactly a lie, what I let you all think. To have said, "Hi, my name is John," would have been the biggest lie.

But the body I've got is mostly wrong still, and the doctors won't give me the operation because they say I'm not serious enough about wanting it. According to their classifications, I should wear makeup and tights and get a boyfriend. I have to keep telling them that's not the kind of woman I am. I've spent too many years pretending already, to want to start all over again.

I did like living in the co-op, more than I showed probably. Most days I was able to forget about the whole man/woman business and just be one of the girls. I'm sorry I cocked it all up in the end (no pun intended).

I just wanted to tell you something, Luce; that's why I'm writing. I just wanted to say (here goes), if I had the right body—if I had any kind of body I was wanting to show or share, or if I could feel much of anything these days—then it would be you I'd want to do it with. You'd be welcome. That's all. I just thought I'd tell you that, because what the hell.

It all happened years ago. I wouldn't believe how many years, except for the date on the letter, which I keep folded up small in a sandalwood box with a couple of other important things, like my grandfather's pipe and an iris from the bouquet Di chucked me at her and Theo's wedding.

These days I have a very normal, happy life, in a two-dykes-and-their-dogs-and-their-mortgage kind of way. I'm not quite so picky anymore, and I don't let myself correct people's grammar, at least out loud. Last I heard, the Welcome was still going, though I don't know anyone who lives there. I wonder, are the potatoes still sprouting down at the back of the garden, the ones I watered with J. J.? I thought I saw her at Pride one year—or the back of her neck, anyway—but I might have been imagining it.

Emma Donoghue

In case this sounds like some kind of doomed first-love story, I should admit that I was grateful there was no return address on that letter. I was young that summer—younger than I knew, it occurs to me now. J. J. must have known that I wouldn't have been able to write back, that I'd have had no idea what to say.

Her letter has gone all shiny at the folds. I don't read it for nostalgia; I prefer not to read it at all. It brings back that bruised, shivery feeling of being in love and making one mistake after another, of waking up to find myself in the wrong story. I keep the letter in my box for any time I catch myself thinking I know the first thing about anything.

The Welcome

about "The Welcome"

I spent eight years living in a low-rent, women-only housing cooperative in Cambridge, England. Eight very happy years, despite the satirical and critical elements of this story! (It's much easier to write about a character's frustration than her content, you see.) The co-op was the first place in the world where I ever felt at home as a lesbian. I liked the communal and feminist principles behind its structure, the unpretentious atmosphere, and the high level of frankness in conversation. But I was also aware what a strange little world it would seem if looked at from the outside.

Two incidents suggested the plot of "The Welcome." Once, when we advertised for new members, a man turned up to be interviewed, and we thought it very strange that he would want to live in a women's space; we assumed he just hadn't read the ad properly.

Also, one of our housemates was very shy about her body, I remember, and about six months after she moved in, a few of us started joking one evening (in her absence) about the fact that she could be a man, for all we knew. Not that this girl was remotely androgynous; we just found it a hilarious idea that a man could have moved into a women-only building without anyone noticing. When I came to think about it afterward, it was more of a sad idea than a funny one. It made me think about the walls of identity that can keep people apart.

So J. J.'s dilemma was my starting point for "The Welcome." But by the time I finished writing it, I was just as interested in Luce's experience—I suppose because by becoming obsessed with someone she doesn't understand, she's only doing what most of us do when we fall in love, especially for the first time. . . .

Emma Donoghue

about Emma Donoghue

Emma Donoghue, Irish novelist, playwright, and historian, is the author of the novels *Hood* and *Stir-fry,* and the collection of brilliantly reimagined fairy tales *Kissing the Witch: Old Tales in New Skins.* Also the editor of *Poems Between Women,* she has seen her work translated into German, Dutch, and Swedish.

Emma Donoghue now lives in Canada.

about Michael Cart

A past president of the Young Adult Library Services Association, MICHAEL CART is well known as an author, critic, and lecturer. His history of young adult literature, *From Romance to Realism*, is used as a text in many college classes. Both his young adult novel, *My Father's Scar*, and his short-story anthology, *Tomorrowland: Ten Stories About the Future*, were selected as American Library Association Best Books for Young Adults. Mr. Cart's column, "Carte Blanche," appears monthly in *Booklist* magazine, and his award-winning cable television interview program, *In Print*, is syndicated nationally.

The winner of the 2000 Grolier Foundation Award for his contribution to the stimulation and guidance of reading by children and young adults, Michael Cart lives in northern California.